BEACON23

BEACON 23

HUGH HOWEY

WILLIAM MORROW
An Imprint of HarperCollins*Publishers*
Boston   New York

First Mariner Books edition 2016

Copyright © 2015 by Hugh Howey

www.harpercollins.com

Library of Congress Cataloging-in-Publication Data is available.
ISBN 978-0-544-83960-1 (hardcover);
ISBN 978-0-544-83963-2 (pbk.)

Interior art by Ben Adams
Book design by Hugh Howey

Printed in the United States of America

23 24 25 26 27 LBC 14 13 12 11 10

For those who suffer alone

1

LITTLE
NOISES

① CHAPTER

They don't prepare you for the little noises. They put you in a centrifuge until you pass out, ride you up and down parabolic curves until you puke your stomach lining, poke you with needles until you know what an addict feels like, and make you learn three fields of physics and get a medical degree while training for triathlons.

But they don't tell you what it's like to live with the clacks and squeaks and little, distant beeps. Or how the deadness of space for light years around can be felt like a great, crushing weight. That silence seems to build and build, like the darkness I saw once in a cave in West Virginia. Darkness you can chew. Darkness you can feel for miles all around you. Darkness you're not sure you'll ever crawl out of.

The silence of deep space is just like that. Which makes the little whirring gizmos in my beacon a nightmarish clatter of nerve-jangling assholes. I hate every one of them. Everything that moves in this place. Every little gear and piezo buzzer and alarm. It's not just that they're discordant, it's that they're unpredictable. And so I spend the gaps in between bracing for them, waiting for them, expecting them. As soon as you loosen up, they hit. Little pricks on my eardrums.

They are devilish bastards, too. Like deer, they seem to know when you hunt for them. I crawl through the duct-like work spaces of my beacon with a flashlight, wire snips, duct tape, and bits of foam. I stalk the fuckers. I set traps, thinking some of the noises are scurrying away from me, that they must be little critters that came on board with a batch of poorly sterilized fruit.

They seem to hear me coming, and the beeps and buzzes go quiet. Scarce as bucks on the first day of open season. As soon as I crawl out, there they are again, making a racket. Like that same ten-point buck, the day after season, standing in your yard, chewing your tulips with that idiot look on his face, like, "Whut?"

Yeah, I'm coming for you motherfuckers. I've set traps. Microphones with recorders to nail down the locations of the beeps. Squirts of oil everywhere for the squeaks. And every kind of cockroach hotel made for the clickety-clack, moving little noises.

NASA would be proud of my efforts and ingenuity, right? All that training. For this. But what else am I gonna do? I'm the meaty center of this rusted metal popsicle out here on the edge of space. I'm here because they haven't made a computer yet that won't do something stupid one time out of a hundred trillion. Seems like good odds, but when computers are doing trillions of things a day, that means a whole lot of stupid. And I'm supposed to be smart enough to sort them out.

Most of my time not spent hunting down squeaks and creaks is spent up in the lighthouse. I know that's not what we're supposed to call it, but c'mon. At the long end of a tunnel that stands off the rest of the beacon, there's a small cavity with portholes on all sides. The gravity wave broadcaster is in this puppy. It's the business end of the beacon; everything else is just here to make sure it stays running, and that includes me.

The long arm sets the GWB apart from the rest of the beacon because its waves fall off with the fourth power of distance. Those waves will scramble the wires of anything within a five or six meter radius, including mine. NASA advises not spending too much time around the GWB, because it does funny things to your head. Which is another way of saying it gives you a nice mellow. But what do they expect us to do when they post us two years at a time out here in the middle of nowhere? I doubt I'm the only one who sits with my back to the machine, letting it soothe my head like a straight-up whiskey while I gaze out at the dull gray stones of the asteroid field that makes an awful mess of astral navigation.

Across from the GWB, and right above the best porthole for watching the asteroids twirl in space, there's a faded picture that some former resident put up, which is why I suspect I'm not the only one who sits here. In the picture, a man in slickers is standing outside an actual, Earth-based lighthouse. A wave taller than the lighthouse looms behind him, must be twenty meters high. The wave is slamming into this tapered pillar of stone, and you figure it's the last shot of the lighthouse and the man, that this tidal wave utterly destroys both of them in the next fraction of a second, and that the man is smoking his pipe and squinting up at what must be a drone with a camera or something, like he's thinking, "That's the most curious thing," and has no idea his ticket is about to get punched from behind.

I've spent more time looking at this poster than I have at the field of stars and rocks out the window. For a while, I assumed it was computer generated. You can never tell with these things. Sometimes the real looks fake, especially when you've looked at the fake for so long. But why would anyone hang up some CGI with such reverence? The paper is slick, not like the thermal crap we print on here. And there's not a crease on it, which means it was brought flat packed or in a courier roll. Either way, someone took some care in getting it here. So I assume the damn thing is real. I assume this guy is real, that he's having his last toke there at the end of his tiny world and his tiny life.

I get a good gwib buzz staring at this photo, sometimes for hours, while I wait for a CPU to need a reboot or some ship to come out of hyper and ask for directions or give me some news of the war. This man is taking a maelstrom with a shrug and a deep drag like he's such a boss. Such a cool customer. Meanwhile, I lose my shit over some distant, infernal clicking sound. That lighthouse keeper was my hero for the longest time. Until I learned more about that photo.

Turns out there's a dozen variants of similar shots. And yeah, they're all real. I sent a research request to Houston after I couldn't turn up anything in the archives, and I could easily imagine the conversation on their side, because I'd had my share of them when I worked ground support during training:

Chief of Ops: "I'm sorry, 23 wants to know what?"

"Uh, sir, he wants the history behind a particular photo. And no, it's not a spectral chart. Or anything . . . uh, scientific. It's . . . well, here. He sent a digital cap."

Long pause while the Chief stares at a handlet.

"You've gotta be fucking kidding."

"Nossir."

"And he used a *research request* on this? Has he got any left?"

"First one he's ever used, sir. Guy has a clean record. Served on the front before he got his red badge and was reassigned."

"Lemme guess: blow to the head?"

"Nossir. Had his guts clawed out by a Lord. Was given a quiet beacon out on the edge of sector eight."

"So he's probably hugging that GWB like she's some dollar hooker at the end of two tours."

"Probably, sir. Would be my guess."

"Ah, fuckit. The boy's a war hero for crissakes. See what you can dig up."

Of course, that's probably *not* how it went down. Some lackey most likely got the request, Binged that shit himself instead of sending it to the actual research department, and fired off eight pages of search page results and their targets back to me. Probably took him two seconds. I got the response three months later from a tug grabbing an ore load that didn't belong to them. Said they had something for me, then went into the belt and took billions of dollars of something for themselves. It's a crazy world out here on the edge, but enough shrugging and looking the other way, and it all seems to sort itself out.

And as it turns out, my goddamn hero-of-the-mist lighthouse keeper was just as batshit scared as the rest of us. The whole history of that photo is well documented. The shot was from a manned helo, of all things. While the photog was grabbing the pic, the onboard pilot was waving his fool head off for the old lighthouse keeper to *move. Move!* Supposedly, just after he got his picture taken looking like a complete granite badass, the old man was shitting his drawers, dropping his stogie, and leaping through the lighthouse door just in time to save his ass from getting washed away.

This is the thing about being a hero: *It's all about when you get your picture taken.* I'll be a hero for the rest of my life, I suppose. So long as I spend it in here with the door shut, hugging my knees, and staying away from any more cameras.

CHAPTER

My twelfth level of hell consists of a small steel marble dropped from a height of two inches, smacking a solid block of concrete.

That's what it sounds like anyway: the worst of the little random clicks that only come out when I'm in my bunk, trying to sleep. This one particular noise is like a cockroach. Not that it sounds like one—that's the other noises—just that it only scurries out to play when I shut the interior lights off, and then it disappears when I'm up and moving about. My footsteps literally scare it away. Explain that to me.

NASA says everything in the beacon is necessary, that if I'm hearing a noise, it's just a gizmo doing its job. The subtext here is for me to shut the hell up and just do *my* job. Heh. Maybe me and every other beacon operator drive Houston nuts with all our squeaks and requests. Maybe this is them getting back at us. I can see the scene down in

Mission Control right now: a man in a white shirt and black tie checking my vitals on a readout, his chief inquiring if I've hit REM sleep yet.

"Affirmative, sir. Sleeping like a baby."

"Excellent. Queue up the machine that goes *bing!*"

Or the machine that sounds like a steel marble impacting concrete.

This little jewel in my trillion-dollar watchwork beacon is giving me fits while I spin around in my bunk, looking for a pocket of cool and a period of silence. And this is when a different sound reminds me that sounds can be *truly* bad. Not just annoying, not just discordant symphony to my carefully orchestrated silence, but a sound like the *old* sounds, like plasma fire and shard grenades, like suicidal orders from men too slow, old, and wise to wear a jocksuit, noises like bombs going off and air raid sirens. *Those* kinds of noises.

I know what it is the moment I hear it: complete GWB failure. The beacon going dark. I know, because I've run through the simulator beacon in the Mojave a bajillion times. I know, because those simulations still give me nightmares—nightmares with gray-bearded faces peering in through flimsy fake portholes while I try to figure out how they fucked me over this time.

We used to have a joke at SIMCOM: NASA screws its 'nauts up the bum when we're Earthside, because in space, no one can hear you squeal.

GWB failures don't happen. The redundancies have redundancies have redundancies. It gets all incestuous up in beacon 23's innards, I'm telling you. In order for something to go wrong, an alarm has to be out, and a backup alarm, and two different modules built to do the same thing and checked every few seconds to make sure they're capable of doing that thing. All the chips and software are self-healing and able to reboot on their own. You could set off an EMP in this bastard, and she'd be back up in two shakes. What you'd need is two dozen random breakdowns to strike at once, plus a host of other coincidences too mind-boggling to consider.

Some brainiac at NASA calculated the odds once. They were very, very small. Then again, as of last week, there were 1,527 GALSAT beacons in operation across the Milky Way. So I guess the odds of something happening to *someone* keep going up. Especially as the beacons get older. And now I guess that someone is me.

With this little snafu, the noises are suddenly *hoping* to be found. They're calling for me, little alarms everywhere. I scramble from my bunk and climb the ladder to the command module in my boxers. The first thing I check is the power load, and all is kosher. I check the nav gyros and the starfield scanners, and the beacon's not confused about where we are. I check the quantum tunneler, but there aren't any messages. While I'm there, I put in a quick note to Houston, even though I'm sure they're getting an auto relay with error codes out the wazoo.

Outage. 0314 GST.

The beacon will have already warned them, but at least they'll know I'm up. Their man on the scene. The chewy meat center of their big ol' spacesicle.

I grab the edge of the tunnel that leads to the lighthouse and launch myself down the chute toward the GWB in the distance. Done this so many times, I just have to brush a finger against the wall to course correct. Red lights pulse up and down the length of the chute. There's an alarm screaming ahead.

Spreading my arms, fingertips squeaking across metal to slow my arrival, I grab the last rung and swing into the lighthouse.

The GWB is cool to the touch. That means she's not emitting her safe passage corridor to transiting ships. Nor is she being her usual, soothing self. It's like a favorite lager has transmuted into an energy drink. "You're starting to stress me out," I tell her, pulling the hexagonal panels off one by one.

I set them aside and study the smooth dome beneath. There's a clacking somewhere, like a loose bolt tumbling into a recess. I check all the thumbscrews and don't see any missing. More of the random noises. At the base of the GWB, I check all the wires and connections. The first things we're trained to try are the same things I assume we would try without the trillion-dollar education. I begin unplugging everything. Count to ten. Plug it all back in. Make sure everything's seated properly.

In the back of my mind, while doing all this, I'm thinking of shipping schedules. There's a clock on the wall, a brass one that has to be wound once a week or it'll stop working. Anything on batteries up here or with a CPU is toast with the GWB on. I stopped winding the clock when the small sounds started driving me crazy, because I couldn't take the ticking anymore. My guess is it's been five minutes since my note to NASA, so probably right around 0320. There's an 0330 cargo out of Orion, bound for Vega, if I remember correctly. Crew of eight, probably, on a ship that size. And then the beacon seems to spin around me and I have to brace myself as I think about the *Varsk*. An 0342 luxury line transit. What does she carry, five thousand passengers? Plus crew?

I leave the panels off the GWB and thrust down the chute again. Terrible trajectory. I crash into one wall, my bare shoulder skidding, squeaking, burning, which causes me to career and tumble and bang my head and my shin before I arrest myself. "Calm down," I tell myself. "One thing at a time." This is what I used to say out loud when I was a soldier, when doing things too fast could get your guts blown out.

Pulling myself down the chute's handholds, I pick up momentum again in the zero-gee. When I hit the edge of gravity leaking from the beacon proper, I turn and float feet-first, falling the last meter and landing in a crouch.

The power station is two flights down. I skid down the ladder, zipping past the living quarters, palms burning. The clang of bare feet on metal grate. The main relays are nasty cusses, large T-bars with rubber grips. The best way to throw them is to do it with your legs. I squat down, get a shoulder braced under one side of the T, and strain upward, spinning the bar ninety degrees, while unseen contacts on the other end of the bar lose connection.

I repeat this with the other relay. There's a deep *thump* from the cut power, and the room goes full blackout. Emergency battery lights flicker on as their photosensors startle at the void. I count to ten again, letting the power drain from the system, all those little capacitors that can keep a memory of whatever's ailing the processors. I want them to forget. When they power back up from a hard reset, they should restore themselves to factory conditions. Little newborn babes.

The relays are harder to turn back on, now that the T-bars are vertical. I brace a foot on a railing and give a good tug. There's a twinge of pain in my belly from being a hero once. I remember a SIMCOM test years ago, making sure I could turn these relays ten times, back and forth, and thinking my guts were going to spill out of my knotted scars. I remember telling the graybeards after: "Nope, feels great. Never better." Then pissing red for a week.

The lights come back with the first relay. I throw the second. There are no alarms. Everything is rebooting, circuits sorting themselves according to protein-based memories, software reloading from hardwired references. I'm mostly upset at my sleep having been disturbed, and I'm not looking forward to the paperwork and error logs I'll need to wade through.

Up the ladder now, sweating, feet hurting, wishing I'd put on my boots, I check the time. 0326. Two minutes or so for a full reboot. Leaves two minutes of margin for the Orion cargo. Cutting it damn close. I'm thinking about the cargo bound for Vega, and the mess a wreck like that will make for the asteroid field. But it's the *Varsk* that's haunting me. There are five thousand souls watching in-flights right now with their earbuds in. Laughing at that comedy. Ordering another gin and tonic. Snoring. Fumbling for their seats in the darkness as they return from the head. A baby crying, someone sneezing and scaring the hell out of everyone else with that crowded, recycled air.

There's a chime from the QT. A message from Houston. I go over to the screen to read it, but before I get there, the alarms go off again. Screaming at me. The red lights, throbbing. Full GWB failure a *second time*. After a hard reboot.

The impossibility of this is banging against my skull as I stare at the words on the QT, the message from NASA. I blink, but they don't go away. I'd hoped for some solution, something like help up in this joint. Instead, all I get from them is:

What outage?

CHAPTER

3

99% of my time working with NASA is spent bitching that I know more than they do. The other 1% of my time is spent trembling, pissing myself, realizing I might actually be right. Now is one of those latter times. Houston should know everything wrong with my beacon, *especially the fact that it is no longer doing the beacon-like things beacons are built for.*

Instead, I've got someone sipping tepid coffee down in the land of women and pizza checking his readouts and telling me there's nothing amiss. *When I goddamn know something is amiss.* The GWB was cool to the touch. And the alarms are going off again.

I type another quick text. The QT works with entangled particles, and they're destroyed as they're used, but I don't care about budgets right now so much as not wasting time with whatever dweeb can't do his job. I also very purposefully employ the caps button, because they can, in this way, hear us scream in space:

GWB FULL FAIL. ZERO TRANSMIT. CARGO AND LUX LINER IN TRANSIT. HARD REBOOT NO GOOD.

Get on the job, Houston.

I try to imagine people down on Earth stiffening at their consoles, rubbing the sleep from their eyes, and fixing all of this for me remotely, but I know there's not even enough time for another reboot, not before the transit. Not sure why, but I launch back down the barrel to the GWB. Maybe just to watch, to hope nothing happens, to see the complete lack of wake as a ship passes by at twenty times the speed of light.

The GWB is still lifeless and cold when I arrive, the alarms still flashing and blaring. I turn to the porthole facing the asteroid belt—and a new star blooms into a brief and ugly existence. A blinding flash of light. Streaks of molten metal like meteors. An expanding cloud of titanium tinsel. Asteroids crashing and tumbling and knocking into one another, cleaving into smaller hunks of rock. An immense amount of destruction, all without making a sound, a macabre ballet and light show.

A large chunk of the cargo vessel flips end over end, twisted like taffy, great black gouges down the side, and everywhere are the scraps of bright red and blue and gray containers, all their contents spilling into the vacuum of space, much of it pulverized beyond recognition.

It all happens in an instant. None of the destruction is there one moment—just quietude and the mingling of hippo-like rocks—and then chaos and burning and death and space litter. This is what it looks like when a billion-ton spacecraft goes from FTL to slamming into a rock the size of a small county. When the beacon's GWB went out, it was like the street sign before a sharp curve had been removed, the one that warns of the approaching cliff. I think of the eight crewmembers dead. Eight is the number of men in a special battalions squad. We don't normally lose them quite this fast. Oftentimes, one will crawl away and die a slow and lonely death on the edge of space. But no one is crawling away from the disaster beyond my porthole. And five thousand more lives are inbound at twenty times the speed of light.

4

CHAPTER

The archives deep in the heart of beacon 23 house practically every novel ever written. A random trip through the database is an exercise in frustration, as for every one novel I would enjoy, there are roughly three billion I can't get through, and no way of telling the two types apart other than a miserable chapter or two.

Which is why I spend more time reading through the complete Wiki, circa 2245, not updated in several decades, but close enough for solar nukes and frag grenades.

My curiosity over the picture of the lighthouse keeper and the tidal wave led me deep into the Wiki searching for answers, to no avail. But before I reached out to NASA with a research request, I stumbled upon an article that beggared belief. This article comes to mind as I watch the remnants of an interplanetary cargo vessel disperse across the cosmos. It comes to mind as I see what looks like two smaller pirate-class cargo vessels moving out there among the lifeless rocks and the tinsel of torn hull. The article was about an old profession long since lost. Or so the Wiki thought.

In the days of sea-bound ships, when hulls were made to keep water rather than vacuum out, and hazards to navigation were submerged rocks, not the floating-in-space kind, there was a dishonest profession of men known as *wreckers*.

I wouldn't have believed it, were it not right there in the Wiki, but wreckers did just as their name implied: they wrecked ships for a living. A brutal, murderous living.

I increased the zoom on the porthole and watched the flame of thrusters and the white puff of attitude controllers as the two black-painted cargo ships scooted from cargo container to cargo container. And the extreme coincidence of my GWB failure slid away. This was a lighthouse I was standing in, and lighthouses were not always appreciated.

Four or five centuries ago, a lighthouse would go up and down long before it went around and around. That is, some of the lighthouse would get built during the day, and then at night, many of those same stones would disappear. This would go on for months, until the builders posted guards and gave out beatings to the saboteurs. Lighthouses, you see, were bad business for the men who relied on wrecks for a living.

Wrecking probably starts with the sudden and unexpected bounty of one big catastrophe at sea. Lucky and enterprising salvagers sell the spoils that wash up beyond the reef. Before too long, clever and desperate men begin wishing for the next great crash. And so they proceed to make it happen.

In small boats, they offer to guide visiting ships through the reefs, only to take their shallow drafts over rocks that mean doom for the bigger ships. Or they light fires to show harbors that don't exist. They forge sea charts. They rig chains across channels. The lives lost are of less consequence than the spoils gained. In every wreck and crash, there is some unseen man rubbing his hands with thoughts of tidy profits.

Lighthouses, then, are not to be tolerated. NASA *hates* it when we refer to beacons as lighthouses. Maybe they don't want to give any deplorable types any deplorable ideas.

In the distance, beyond my beacon, in a realm of space where I can go weeks without seeing another living soul, I watch some such deplorable people go about their business, and I'm powerless to stop them. I'm also reminded that there's no such thing as coincidences. My little lighthouse on the edge of sector eight was taken down, brick by brick.

I shove away from the porthole and down the barrel again, needing to tell Houston. "We have a problem," I hear myself thinking. But no one writes that anymore. We *only* get in touch with Houston when we have a problem. No point in wasting entangled particles on the redundant.

Sabotage, I type into the QT. There's no all-caps. Watching the cargo explode into countless pieces, and the equivalent of a squad die at the hands of pirates, has left me numb. *Reboot unsuccessful.* I backspace and change to *Reboot failed. Please advise.*

I hit "send." Then "confirm." And finally: "Yes, I'm sure."

The machine beeps. At least it's a good little noise. So much of the beacon must've been fucked with all at once, including the QT error reporting to Houston. And this is when the big realization hits me like a sack of bricks. This is when my months-long torment with the little sounds makes me feel less insane. In the minutes since I realized my beacon has been hacked by wreckers, I've assumed it was done from the outside. Some way of getting around NASA's supposedly iron-tight security measures. Some brilliant hack.

Then I think about a trade I made with some unseemly characters a while back. I think about the other ship that dropped off my research request and then proceeded to steal ore from the belt. In the days of wooden ships, pests came on with boxes of fruit. Cockroaches hatched from eggs laid in cardboard. Rats found their way into the bilges, where they had more rats. What the fuck have I done?

I think of the sounds that seemed to scurry out of the way whenever I got near. And suddenly, I'm not alone in the beacon. I scan the walls of knobs and displays. There are pipes running everywhere around me, bundles of wire drooping from the ceiling, open panels from recent projects that allow me to peek into the innards of NASA's little creation. And the creepy-crawlies are everywhere. Watching me. Little metal insects that don't get caught in my traps, because they're the wrong kind of traps.

I check the time. Ten minutes before the *Varsk* passes these waters. Waters. Taking the imagery too far. Or maybe it's because I feel like I'm drowning. Back in the war zone. A medal pinned to my chest in a hospital, pinned there for saving a fraction of the lives that are about to be lost because of me. There won't be any photos of this. Just headlines of an accident. Five thousand dead. And I'm still a hero, smoking my pipe, that awful wave reaching up behind me.

The QT beeps with a message from NASA.

Sitrep

"Situation report?" I ask the void. I say to the creepy crawlies, to no one in particular: "Situation normal, motherfuckers. I screwed up."

I bang my palm on the screen closest to me, and the green phosphorous readout wavers for a moment. Wreckers. I'll be lucky if they don't kill me. Lucky they haven't already. I need to get a message off to NASA to warn them of future hacks like this. Social hacks are always the easiest way in, because people like me are the weakest link. I don't worry about the QT costs. I hammer out a quick explanation, a best guess:

Took on illicit delivery. Bugs in the shipment, metal kind. Some kind of hack. Took down all the systems at once. Check other beacons. Look into history of Wreckers. Pirates taking cargo. Not sure if they'll fix the beacon. Lux liner with 5k pop heading this way. Reboot may have worked, but they just shut GWB off as soon as it came on.

I hit send. I confirm. But before I can say "I'm sure," I think about my explanation. Is it right? There was definitely a delay before the alarms came on, like maybe the reboot worked but then the GWB was shut down again.

Does that mean the critters are still here, watching me? Is there anything I can do about them?

Staring down the barrel toward the lighthouse, I think of a disinfectant. I think of war, where some lives are lost in order to save others. Where even eradication is a thing we'll consider. Where the greatest evils become the greater goods.

My hand is on my bare stomach, rubbing cords of knotted flesh, the raised welts of scars that tell a story. I stop this. There's no time for that. No time but to act.

CHAPTER

⑤

There's a run of wire overhead to send power out to the red docking target, the big red O that guides in supply ships. I grab this and give it a good yank, pulling it free from its velcro harness. Finding my snips, I hack one end of the wire and tug enough from the chases for what I'll need. I grab a wrench and boost myself down the barrel to the lighthouse.

The GWB is still exposed, its panels lying on the floor. The clock on the wall is showing me the wrong time. I almost wish it were wound, wouldn't mind the ticking. I'd love to know how much time I have left.

I cut the power feeds to the GWB. The voltage for it and the docking lamp are both 220, if I remember the schematics right. Been a while since I had to know this shit. With the wrench, I loosen the six bolts that hold the gravity wave broadcaster dome to its mount, like removing the light fixture from a lighthouse. I get it free and leave the wrench behind. Cradling the GWB like a beach ball, I move slowly down the barrel toward the control room, turning before gravity takes over, landing in a crouch.

I leave the GWB in the middle of the floor, near the coil of wire. Down the ladder and to the fuses again. I put my back into them, and they turn a little more easily, maybe from being worked back and forth already. When the power goes out, I head for the ladder, not waiting for my eyes to adjust or the emergency lighting to come on. Bump and fumble, I'm up two rungs before I can see again. A humming somewhere of power winding down in a pump or a spinning fan. The chiming of my bare feet on the rungs.

I strip the ends of the docking target power cord and splice them to the GWB. The creepy crawlies are watching me. Little metal legs twitching. Infrared cameras curious. Poised by the beacon's relays and electrical inputs with their little instructions to wreck shit. I tell myself this, even though I don't know. Even though I suspect I'm just a little bit crazy. Even though it might all be in my head.

Three minutes. The splices are shit, but should relay enough power. Enough to fry batteries and electronics for a few-meter radius. Any chips not built to handle it. Anything that can't do a hard factory reset.

Back to the power relays, sliding down the ladder with hands and feet on the outer rails. Bruising my heel on impact. Limping over in the glow of the emergency lights. I throw the breakers, imagining old men with gray beards peering in at me through the portholes, watching this idiot ruin their simulation, making notes on their clipboards, shaking their weary heads.

First breaker makes contact, and the lights come on. Then the next. There's a pause while the GWB warms up, then a series of pops and hisses as it fries everything nearby. No time for alarms. Darkness descends. A flickering, unsteady, then absolute darkness.

Back up the ladder now, this time with no lights. Nothing. Just my labored breaths, the slap of palms on the ladder, the ticking of an internal clock, the thought of all those people in that liner, and all the other people I couldn't save. Corpses. Bones. Grinning skeletons. Friends and brothers in combat suits, that befuddled look on faces just before the lights go out inside, even though they know what's happening, even though they've expected it for years since boot camp, even though they've seen it before with their buddies, but the last part that goes is the little sliver of hope that thought you'd get through this mess, that thought you'd live to see the other side, that it'd be your name on the war memoir, on the cover, not in the dedication.

I find the GWB by crawling around and groping in the pitch black. Find the wires. Yank them free. Then crawl back to the ladder to do it all again. Exhausted. Like PT. Forced marches. Don't get enough exercise in this place. My stomach hurts, but it's probably just a stabbing recollection. A painful memory. Nothing more.

I throw the breakers for what I hope is the last time. Another factory reset, all those chips rebuilding themselves, software going back to primitive states, power flickering on, the beeps and whirrings and hissings that are *supposed* to be there.

I wonder if the wreckers anticipated this, if their little bugs have self-healing CPUs. They do or they don't. No time to waste dwelling on it. I'm back up the ladder, my arms quivering, my legs numb, wishing I'd killed the gravity before I started this. That would've been smart. A good soldier would've thought of that.

I grab the GWB and pull myself down the barrel. In the lighthouse, the porthole is still zoomed in on the debris. Motion and activity out there, the motherfuckers. I only tighten two of the bolts before I grab the wires. No time to go back and shut off the power while I juice it up, so I decide to splice it on hot. Negative first, careful not to touch the wires together or to the same metal surface. Then the positive, sparks flying right as they touch, but settling as I wind the copper ends tight to each other.

I sit back. Listen for the hum. Place a hand on the dome. Is it getting warm, or is that my heat? My sweaty palm?

There is no clock. But I know the time is short, and that the only way I'll know if it didn't work is a sudden bloom of light that fills the portholes, another great wreck to sift through, this time full of bodies and all their valuables. I think of the wreckers of old who sorted through wooden chests and gathered planks and coils of rope while corpses washed up on the beach. I see men in zero-gee pulling the boots off the drowned. Digging through pockets. Yanking gold chains from necks. Sucking on lifeless fingers to loosen rings.

Then I see a scared little soldier sitting in a muddy trench on an alien world, finger on the trigger, just needing to shoot. To shoot. The boys all around are shooting, and they're ending up dead. The best thing I ever did in life was nothing, and I got a medal for it. I was a hero once. And if you look at my picture, that's all I'll ever be.

Minutes pass. Hours. I'm sobbing with relief. Nothing happened. Nothing. The unseen wake left by five thousand squirming souls as they pass me by at twenty times the speed of light. On they go, leaving me here, sobbing. Eighteen more months on this shift, alone, my back to the sea, tending to my little beacon with all its pretty little noises.

2

PET
ROCKS

CHAPTER

⑥

When a trans-orbital cargo ship traveling twenty times the speed of light bumps into large, stationary rocks, it makes quite a scene.

I can attest.

I am witness.

According to the labcoats at NASA, I might be the only soul to see such a spectacle with his own eyes and live to tell the tale. Besides the asshole pirates who caused the ruckus in the first place, I have to remind them.

Thinking about the picture of the lighthouse operator up in the business end of my beacon, I find myself wondering if any of those old keepers felt this empty, gnawing, hungry, depressed sensation after a ship was lost on their rocks. I wonder if they felt this helplessness, this dread, this sense of duty derelictioned—if that's even a word. Did they watch for weeks as planks of wood and tangles of rope washed up on their shores? Did they feel as though they didn't do quite enough? That the blood out there was on their hands?

I hope not. I wouldn't wish this on anyone, much as I crave the company, much as I wish I didn't feel so alone. It's a selfish craving, desiring a partner in misery. The brotherhood of war was a lot like this. You didn't want your squadmates to be there, suffering with you, but you couldn't have made it through without them. You wanted them home as badly as they wanted to be home, but only if you all got to go at once. I'm pretty sure every one of us was thinking: *Don't leave a man behind—especially not me.*

It's been seven days since the wreck, and I haven't slept much. I have no appetite. I keep telling myself it was only eight dead, which would've been a great day along the front, but maybe it's the near-miss of the passenger liner that keeps me up at night and has me skipping my morning bowl of protein mix. Even though the passenger ship passed by without incident, I can somehow see five thousand bodies tumbling out there among the rocks. I can hear their families weeping. None of them know how close they came. But I do. I get the shakes when I think about it. I concentrate instead on the four men and two women who *did* die out there, and I run everything over and over in my head, wondering what I could've done differently.

NASA had some choice words, of course. No more trading with ships passing through the system. I am officially on quarantine. Protocols across all the beacons are being affected because of my dumb ass. I remember a morning in flight school when the entire platoon had to run thirty klicks because of some wisecrack I made. I'm still making trouble for everyone else. Before I can stop it, my mind jerks back to my last day in the war, with my squad dead, three platoons hunkered down, oblivion approaching...

I clamp down on those memories. I embrace fresher torments. But my shrink warned me about this, how anger and depression get misassigned, and how if I don't work through shit it'll keep resurfacing in ways I don't expect. Maybe it's not the eight dead or the five thousand saved that have me feeling this way. And maybe taking this job was the worst way possible to wrestle down my demons. They've got me trapped here, in my beacon. And vastly outnumbered.

If my private torments aren't going away anytime soon, at least the cosmos has a short memory. The armada of news ships with their channel stations painted across their hulls has come and gone. As well as the private yacht rubberneckers and souvenir seekers and scavengers. The busted cargo ship was like a spilled can of soda. A swarm of ants and bees came, and now are gone.

NASA, bless them, can only concentrate on the fact that my rebooting the beacon erased the last few hours of recordings from the scanners, and so we have no vid of the disaster. They say I missed a prime opportunity to record just what happens when a ship collides with a meteor field in hyperspace. I might've saved five thousand lives, but the way my bosses are talking, it was too cheap an exchange for what might've been learned.

Funny, I thought I was getting away from such hard calculations when I left the army. I suppose half a klick won on some alien rock has a price about the same as a paragraph gained in the storehouse of human knowledge. Everyone's gonna die anyway, right? Well, someone should explain to these clowns that borders aren't forever either, and neither are their theories. It all goes. They can damn me all they like for choosing to save lives. Guess we each have our own stupid priorities.

•••

I sit with my back to the restored GWB to calm these thoughts. Whatever the dome does to the local gravity field to warn ships of danger, it does something just as useful to my head. I worry less when I'm up here. It's like two fingers of whiskey that keeps tumbling through my veins, never stopping, never subsiding, never becoming too much.

Outside the porthole in front of me, a massive field of debris catches the starlight. The only NASA scanner that remembers what happened is my imperfect and bewildered brain, and it replays the impact in a loop. I see a flash of light, asteroids as big as moons bursting into clouds of bright powder, cargo that survived the impact scattering, the rear half of the massive ship popping out of hyperspace and exploding into countless pieces, and a vortex of bouncing mass and momentum and splintering steel and rock.

I described it all to the labcoats as best I could. I nodded at the animations they came up with. I watched them lumber around my beacon, going through all the panels and crannies, sniffing out the sabotaging little vermin that tormented me with their squeaks and clicks, everyone lecturing me on the new quarantine protocols. As shrapnel and rocks clinked and clanged off the beacon like hailstones, and men smarter than me frowned at whatever they were calculating in their noggins, I wondered if they'd send me home like the army had. But they packed up and went zipping back to Houston, leaving me in this funk.

The debris has kept on striking the beacon since they left, though the patter is becoming more sparse. Ignoring the labcoats' reassurances, I've taken to sleeping in the lifeboat, just in case. I retrieved the walk suit from the airlock—the thing smelling of a decade of sweat and storage—and I wear it all the time now. I sleep with my helmet right in front of me. The first two nights, I slept with the helmet on, the visor closed, my exhalations fogging my vision.

The sight of myself in the mirrored visor isn't pretty, I have to admit. I look like a dead man. Gaunt. Unshaven. Older than my thirty-five years. But I keep the image of myself close at hand, my helmet within reach, just like in my army days. I long ago learned to embrace the illusion that a thin veneer over my skull might save me. No rock to hide under, so this will have to do.

In the middle of the night last night, a whizzing hunk-of-something punched a neat hole in the upper solar array, waking me up and sending me scrambling for a damage assessment. An awful clatter followed as a small storm of debris peppered the hull—but the beacon never lost integrity. I've been keeping an eye on the atmo gauges ever since. The alarms should sound if something goes amiss, but I keep wondering what happens if the alarms are the first things damaged? Or if I'd even hear the alarms in the lifeboat at night. This is like living in the trenches again, just a different kind of bombardment. But there's that nervous, anxious energy every second, that knowledge that your life could end before you have enough time to call out for your momma. Just a whistle, and then a cloud of red. Or in this case, a sharp bang, a hiss of vacuum equalizing, and then a cold, asphyxiating death.

To keep my mind off things, I go over the scans I managed to get of the aftermath. I caught a lot of the debris expanding and ricocheting, and I got great vid of the two scavenger ships that caused the wreck in the first place. Grabbed their signatures and hull IDs before they could zip off into the FTL yonder. I'm sure the sigs are bogus, but it made me feel useful. And with the full zoom on the viz scanner, I can sit and watch the little bastards in their spacesuits as they sift through the drifting cargo, getting what they can, stuffing their holds, then leaving.

Somewhere out there, eight crewmembers are dead and drifting—unless the navy found the bodies or one of the rubberneckers thought a corpse would suffice as a souvenir. Somewhere out there, a bunch of TVs are switching over to news of the war, and how it's edging into sector seven right now, and which planet might fall next. Pretty much everywhere but here, eight dead is old news. Nothing to see. Guess you've got to be pretty lonely to care about the loss of a handful of strangers.

And I suppose my view is shaped by the portholes around me. Eight people probably died from slipping in their showers in the time it took me to have this thought right here of them slipping in their showers. But it's more than the deaths I saw; it's the *destruction*. The noise with which we go seems to make it count for more. I think of my buddies who checked out via hand grenade versus those who died from MRSA back in the VA. We barely notice the latter. They're statistics. Go quietly, and you're a number. Go in spectacular fashion, and you're a *name*.

I never wanted to be a name. I think of how I nearly went out, with the rest of my squad. I think of the people who want to make a movie out of that last stand. The publishers with their book deals. The ghostwriters who clamor to write of ghosts.

Everyone wants me to relive that. I just want to get lost. I asked for a post somewhere where no one would find me, where no one would know my name.

So they gave me a number. 23. My little beacon.

But then the bright flash came for me anyway, and a squad drifts dead in space, and the war is creeping closer.

I can't sleep at night.

And maybe that's a good thing.

(7)

CHAPTER

An alarm is going off up in the command station, four flights away from the airlock wing. I've truly crawled into a hole. Now I climb out to see what in the world is beeping. With the walk suit on, the ladder is a bitch. I climb with one hand, my helmet in the other, thumping up the rungs by my hip. This is me losing my shit. This is NASA's investment in me gone to waste.

I crawl through the power and life support pod, through my old living quarters, and up into what I like to think of as my office. One of the scanners is flashing. I'm lumbering that way when the QT beeps with a message. I decide to check that first, knowing it'll be a message from NASA, probably asking me to check whatever's beeping on the scanner. These little messages from Houston are the only company I have. The contact is nice. Too bad Houston is full of assholes and taskmasters. Maybe prisoners in isolation feel what I feel: they hate their guards, but a beating now and then is at least some human contact.

I check the readout. I am their trained monkey.

Picking up life sig

This seems so unlikely that I assume the station is still glitching from the reboot. A second message beeps through before I can even turn to check the scanner:

Check scanner

"I am," I say. "Jeez."

Sometimes I wish the QT weren't quite so instantaneous.

Letting out a sigh, I cross the command room to check the bio scanner. It's one of the more sensitive instruments on the beacon, and that's saying something. If lichen or viruses start collecting on the outside of the hull, the scanner sounds an alarm, like it's doing right now. I acknowledge the alarm to shut it off, but the light keeps flashing to let me know the reading is still active.

The eggheads in Houston joke that the bio scanner can hear a protein folding in the vacuum of space five hundred klicks away. They think that's funny, because sound doesn't travel through space. At least, I think that's the joke. NASA is weird about the things they fear. They get really nervous about unknown life forms, and yet it's all they talk about. They're like teenage boys with sex in this way.

I study the blip, wishing it would vanish. It's been a week since the crash. Is there any chance one of the crew survived the impact in a stasis pod? Or did a load of produce just now break open when its case smashed into something else?

The signal is definitely out there amid the debris. And a solid target, not a dispersal blip like you might see if a container was leaking biofuels. Something is alive. Or the beacon's scanners are wrecked. I reckon the latter is more likely. I watch the blip and count to ten, waiting for whatever it is to die in the vacuum of space. If the thing were sealed in a suit or a ship, the scanner wouldn't pick up jack. Even with all the activity in the sector lately, the scanner has only gone off briefly, when someone pumps their shitter, and that's just for a flash.

Go away, I tell the blip. *I don't need you.*

. . .

I bite my nails. It's a habit I've mostly given up.

. . .

Mostly.

. . .

Damn. Okay. Back to the QT, where I type: *I see it. 32K*

In other words: Confirmed. And it's thirty-two klicks away, so can we please pretend it isn't there?

Check it

In other words, go out into the vacuum of space, see what's alive out there, and report back if it doesn't kill you first.

Fucking NASA. In a horror movie, when everyone is hugging their shins and shouting for the main character to turn and run, or crawl under the bed, or call the cops, or grab a gun, NASA would be the dude in the back shouting, "Go see what made that noise! And take a flashlight!"

8

CHAPTER

At least I already have on the walk suit, and after a week of sleeping in it, the thing reeks of *my* sweat, not someone else's. It's this positive outlook on life that got me through three and a half tours of duty and the last six months of my first beacon stint. I'm a chipper guy, once you get to know the raw, dark dread and petrified fear that lurks in my breast and that I battle with every waking moment and that sometimes has me sobbing into my palms when no one is around and makes it really hard to be in crowds or to stand any loud sounds and has me thinking I'll probably never be in a functional relationship again, platonic or otherwise. Once you get that, you have to say to yourself, "Hey, why's this guy so damn happy all the time?"

I load a few supplies into the lifeboat (medkit, extra tank of O2, all-in-one meal, jug of water) and make sure the sampling case is locked in its compartment. Running checks on the engines and life support reminds me of my piloting days, back before I got grounded and forced into infantry. Drunks are an asset on the front line, the army taught me. In the air, we're a nuisance.

As I'm warming the thrusters and wondering what's alive out there in the asteroid field, I find myself craving a laser pod or two under my wings. And then I have to remind myself that this rusting bucket doesn't even *have* wings. She's shaped like an outhouse—only doesn't smell as nice. She flies like crap, too, I am reminded, as I seal the hatch and decouple from the beacon. I maneuver with a wobble until I get a feel for the stick. Craning my neck, I look back at my little home in outer space, and the sight of her gives me vertigo.

I live in that?

The beacon is just an off-white can in an oil slick of black. Char marks and black spots dot the hull from micro impacts, and I can see a star through the new hole in the upper solar array. Flashing lights on the top and bottom of the beacon and out on the edges of the arrays signal a hazard to navigation to no one in particular. My sector is empty, save for the beacon. Even the bulk of the wreckage is gone; only the curls of metal and tinsel of carbon fiber indicate that anything happened here, like an intersection after a car crash with its scattering of glass and broken taillight covers.

I should get out more, I realize. The perspective feels good. NASA regs state that we should go for a walk once a week to inspect things, but I'm told no one does that. It's easier to sit with our heads against the GWB, enjoying the buzz and hoping nothing bad happens to stir us from our miserable comfort.

The multi-display on the dash flickers as I lose uplink with the beacon for a moment. I slap the side of the unit, and the video returns to normal. I've got the beacon's bio scanner repeating to the display so I can track the blip. I keep waiting for it to disappear. I can feel my beacon operator down in Houston tracking all the telemetry and drumming their fingers on their desk, wishing I'd hurry up and get them more data. At the neighboring desk, an operator is probably dealing with beacon 512 and a pesky blackwater pump with a mind of its own. Next row down, someone is telling beacon 82 that their traffic lane is being diverted, and a tug will be out next week to relocate them. Suddenly, Houston is nothing more than a customer support call center, tending to the small emergencies across a fleet of expensive metal drums that dot the expanse of the cosmos. Heh. Maybe *we're* the taskmasters, not them.

The collision alarm sounds as a large asteroid tumbles and spins my way. It's a long way off, plenty of time to correct course, but as I do so, I can see why the alarm has given me so much notice: this tin can drives like a unicycle, and the lone wheel is that spinny one on the shopping cart with a mind of its own.

Around the back side of a small moon of a rock, about thirty klicks from the beacon, I get a lock on the bio source. It's just five hundred meters ahead, and it's drifting toward the beacon at a decent clip. Like it was coming for me. I reach to zoom the HUD for a visual and find my gloved hand pawing at empty space. There is no HUD. I'm not in my Falcon. Crazy how long little twinges of habit like this can last. I have to make do with leaning forward against my harness to strain with my eyes.

There.

Among the maze and jumble of rocks, an object with neat manmade lines and corners. Looks like a standard cargo container, the kind that gets loaded into the belly of short-hop atmo ships in those busy cargo spaceports above settled planets. She's painted bright green and has marks of impact across her side, along with writing in a few different languages.

I slow the lifeboat—little crystals forming from the forward jets of air—and unfold the articulating arm that tucks in under her nose. As I get closer, I see a constellation of objects drifting alongside the container—its contents, no doubt spilled after a collision with one of the many tumbling rocks. A toilet seat spins past. Dozens of them. Splinters of wooden crates. Gossamer moths of ladies' dresses, many still on hangers, oddly keeping their wrinkled shapes as they drift past.

I enter an asteroid field within an asteroid field. If the larger assemblage of rocks represents some proto-planet that never quite formed, then this is like a department store that never achieved critical mass.

Turning the lifeboat toward the container, I flip on the forward spotlights, which barely pierce the dark interior of the metal box. I wonder, briefly, if I'm going to have to go in there. And it occurs to me that until someone licks AI, this is why NASA needs monkeys in space. To make stupid monkey decisions like these.

I check the multi-display again to see what the bio scanner is telling me. The signature looks different. More faint. I slap the screen and the entire image wavers, but the little red blip in the center remains a shadow of its former self. Whatever was alive out there won't be for much longer. And now that I'm here, so close to whatever it is, I feel the need to rescue it. I just wanted it to go away before. Now I want it to hold out a little bit longer.

I turn the ship from side to side and watch the blip. That helps to triangulate it, to make sure the source is coming from inside the container. A large plastic postal service bin tumbles past, spilling envelopes and small packages. There are more of the damn toilet seats. They clunk off the hull, but pose no threat. And the red blip slips to the side of the screen. Somehow, it has moved past me.

Turning the ship, I watch the screen until the blip is centered again. I peer at the spot and see only the small cluster of packages and mail items. So I won't be rescuing anyone. It was a silly fantasy anyway. What I'm probably tracking down is a batch of cookies from someone's grandmother, cookies that have now grown hairy with space-resistant mold. A letdown for me, though NASA goes bonkers for mold, so my operator will be thrilled.

A dozen meters from the assemblage, I unfold the articulating arm. I open my visor to see better and release my harness so I can lean forward and peer through the windshield. Using the arm, I gently wave back and forth through the trail of packages, knocking them on new trajectories. I keep glancing down at the screen to see when the blip moves. But when I see the object with my own eyes, I know. Somehow, I know. Through a torn cardboard package, I see a wooden box, bigger than a toaster, rich red like cherry, and gleaming with varnish.

It's not just the vivid beauty of the object, caught in the lifeboat's spotlights, nor the grain of wood—a sight for sore eyes. It's the way the box has broken open that makes me think the sign of life picked up by the sensors might be leaking from the ruptured package.

I pass through a haze of envelopes and bound packages. Reaching with the arm, I seize the box, and then I turn the lifeboat ninety degrees; the blip stays perfectly centered on the screen. This is the object that disrupted the reverie of my day. Its signal is faint and fading. I close my visor and pull the articulating arm back inside, bringing whatever I've found into the safety and comfort of my atmosphere.

CHAPTER

9

I wait to inspect the box in the airlock, back at the beacon. If there's any contamination, I can purge the airlock and decontaminate myself before entering the living space or removing my suit. I'm not hopeful though. The blip of life on my display was already fading fast when I brought the object inside. I'm starting to think someone's order for a pet frog or worms to go fishing with was cracked open when that container took a tumble.

I set the box down on the changing bench in the airlock and drop the medkit satchel on the floor. Rummaging through the medkit, I find the biogen scanner. There's a massive red warning stamped on it: "DO NOT REMOVE HELMET BEFORE USE." Which makes me think they should have the warning on the inside of our visor, not on the scanner. By the time you're reading this warning, you've already acted responsibly. I fumble with the infuriatingly little power switch on the scanner, wondering how many space monkeys have removed their thick gloves before operating this thing and how bad a job NASA does at creating and placing warnings.

It finally powers up. I wave the scanner over my suit, around my helmet, up and down my arms, then slowly bring it toward the box. I orbit the box twice. I can feel the scanner humming in my palm. An amber light flashes while it takes its readings, and then, finally, the light goes green.

Green means everything is okay. At least, I'm pretty sure that's what it means. Or does green mean, *Yes, we found something hazardous*? No, that wouldn't make any sense. I'm just second-guessing because this is scary shit, and I remind myself that if there was anything in the air that would react with my body, it would've reacted with the scanner. What I really want right now is a second scanner to scan *this* scanner. And maybe a third.

My hibernating little OCD self seems to be stirring. He only does this when he's pretty sure I'm about to die a horrible, grisly death. I saw a lot of this guy in the war. But during the last week, he's been that old college roommate who just drops in one day, crashes on the couch, and next thing you know he's living with you and leaving the milk out on the counter.

Ah, fuck it. I either die in the airlock breathing in some toxin being mailed to a politician, or I sit around until a large hunk of debris punches a hole in the wall, sucking out every bit of my atmosphere. I debate whether or not to hold my breath. Is the massive, wheezing inhalation that follows worse than all the small little puffing breaths I might take instead? (I often debated this when a squad mate would lay a fart with a howl of laughter. Breathe normal? Or put it off and then risk sucking that fart so deep into your lungs that it stays there forever, little fart cells melding way inside the core of you?)

I go with the sipping breath technique, lips pursed, almost whistling as I breathe in little gasping bits of air. Trusting that damn scanner, I pop my visor. The breathing technique makes me a little dizzy. At least, I think it's the breathing. My OCD roommate is screaming in my skull, yelling, "Told you so!" and assuring me we're both about to die and that it's all my fault for not listening to him.

I pop my helmet and tug off my gloves. I breathe more normally, and the dizziness subsides. My roommate shrugs, munches on a cold slice of pizza, and turns back to the TV. I return my attention to the little box.

There's a pair of shears in the medkit for cutting gauze and snipping away walk suits. I use these to cut the cardboard box that's still partially concealing the gleaming wood. I'm careful not to destroy the label, as I'm sure NASA will want to know who the package was going to and where it was coming from. Glancing at the name, I see that it was heading to a university on Oxford. The initials are SAU. Never heard of it. But there are only a few thousand universities on Oxford, and I could probably name two. The recipient is a Prof. Allard Bockman. The sender's name was damaged by the impact, but I'm sure NASA will be able to track the barcode.

I set the cardboard aside and study the box, which is gorgeous even in its damaged state. An ornate pattern carved around the perimeter looks like a chain of links, all intertwined. It's imperfect enough for me to imagine it was done by hand, but it's precise enough that I recognize the talent and care put into it. Or maybe a machine made it with just enough variation to fool me into thinking it was done by hand. You never know what's real these days. How do cynics find joy in even the simplest of things anymore?

The first thing I inspect is the damage. I probe the destroyed corner with my thumb; there are jagged splinters everywhere. It occurs to me, suddenly—my roommate drops his slice of pie and jumps from the couch in alarm— that the hole may have been created from within, rather than punched from without. Maybe something escaped!

I set the box down and take a step back, nearly tripping over my helmet. For a moment, out of the corner of my eye, one of my gloves looks like a giant white spider. I shriek. I remember the fear I used to feel in the army from seeing a sword-leech in my bunk—and then the much greater fear from *no longer seeing the sword-leech in my bunk*—and electricity rushes up my spine.

There's an itch by my knee.

And something moving along my hip and up my ribs.

I claw at the suit I haven't taken off for a week, trying to remember where the buckles and zippers and snaps are. Working my arms and legs free, I realize the itching is probably from having the damn thing on for a week, and that I've been itching constantly for days. And that the only thing likely to kill me in that suit is the damn stench.

Naked and sweating, breathing hard, a hundred thousand dollars' worth of NASA garb inside out and scattered like a tux on a wedding night, I try to remember a guy who used to pick up a rifle and run toward a legion of Ryph with balls of plasma blooming on either side of him, eruptions of dirt, dogfights in the atmo, and kinetic missiles zipping down from orbit.

Who is this limp-dick, shell-shocked, mamby-wamby space monkey I've become?

Was this me before boot camp?

This was me back in high school. The real me. What the hell did the army do to me?

That's when I hear the scratching noise. Coming from the box sitting on the airlock bench.

And a small voice that does not seem to be coming from inside my head.

CHAPTER ⑩

Picking up the box, that mirror finish of wood with the hole blown out, I turn it to find the clasp, and again I hear something move inside. I feel the clunk of something heavy hitting one wall of the box. I feel it vibrate slightly in my hand.

The clasp is really a series of four wood pegs, each bigger around than my finger. I push them in one at a time, and when I push the fourth, it causes the first three to slide back out flush with the box. I push the first three in again, but the lid won't open. I reset them. Try the first two. Reset. The first and third. Reset. The middle two. Reset. Just the first. Reset. Just the second. And the lid pops open.

The thing inside shifts again. And then I hear someone say:

"Jesus Christ on a popsicle stick, took your goddamn time."

There is a rock inside the box.

I look at the rock.

I feel like the rock is looking at me.

The rock shifts position ever so slightly.

"What?" it asks.

"Hello?" I say.

"Yeah, hello, what the hell took you so long? I was dying in here."

"You're . . . a rock," I tell the rock.

"The fuck I am."

I set the box back on the bench and rest on my heels, peering at the little thing. It's gray with deep pockets of black, little fissures and cracks and pockmarks. One of the black spots is deep and might be an . . . eye? I've gone through countless flashcards of alien life for the army and NASA, and I've forgotten most of what I had to memorize to get through the tests, but I know there are shitloads of creatures that camouflage themselves either to not get stepped on or to kill the fuck out of those of us who step too close to them. Yet I've never seen a creature that looks so much like . . . a rock.

"What are you?" I ask.

"Well, since you're obviously a human, you'd call me an Orvid. And since your accent places you from Earth, you'd obviously not give a fuck what I call myself in my own tongue, so why bother?"

"You're a foul-mouthed thing," I say.

"This is me shrugging like I give a shit," the rock tells me.

"This is weird," I say out loud, mostly to myself, but I guess partly to the rock. "I mean, a lot of my life has been really freaking kooky and batshit crazy, but this is fascinatingly weird."

"Yeah, no shit. I'm on my way to a happy life in Oxford, and next thing I know I can't breathe and some fruitloop is shrieking and shaking my happy little wooden home and giving me hell for my vocabulary. Jesus, man, I almost just died, and you're thinking about yourself? What kind of special selfish *are* you?"

This brings me up short. My brain is still whirling with the idea that this rock-looking alien is actually alive, so I haven't considered the fact that a clearly sentient being very nearly just died, and here I am worried about my own feelings.

"Damn," I say. "Sorry. Totally. Are you okay? You need . . . like little pebbles to munch on or something?" I laugh.

"Fuck you," the rock says. "What I need is some water."

•••

This is me, in a beacon, out on the edge of sector eight, so damn near the edge that I might as well be in sector nine, running the tap on my moisture reclamator, filling a plastic cup with water, then drizzling it on top of a rock in a smashed wooden box.

"Not on my fucking head!" the rock says.

I apologize but laugh. The rock has what sounds vaguely like a British accent, which makes everything it says funnier than it should.

"Sorry," I say.

"Just a little puddle, man. And save me some time by putting me in it."

I do this. It occurs to me that I haven't called this in or checked with NASA about what I found. I go over to the

QT to see if there are any messages. Nothing. That's pretty damn curious. So I fire off a quick "55" to Houston, which is beacon code for "Everything here is hunky-dory, in case you were wondering."

"Where are we?" the rock asks. And I realize that I need a name for the guy. And how really fucking cool it is to have some company other than my freaked-out OCD roommate.

"Beacon 23," I say. "Sector eight. On the outer edge of the Iain Banks asteroid field, between the ore rim and—"

"Yeah, jeez, okay. The middle of nowhere, I get it. So when's the next pickup?"

"The next what?"

"WHEN DO I GET HOME?" the rock shouts. It sounds like a little squeal more than a great roar, like a piece of chalk on a blackboard.

"The, uh, next supply shuttle will be in . . . I think three months?"

The rock stares at me.

Did he just shrug?

He looks exasperated.

A bubble forms on the surface of his little puddle.

I wonder if rocks can fart.

"I need to name you," I tell the rock.

"The hell you do."

"I'm thinking . . ."

"Already got a name," the rock says.

". . . oh, but that's too obvious." I laugh. I laugh hard. It's the first time I've laughed in so long that all my emotional triggers, which have only known sobbing, mix some tears in with the laughter.

"Don't you fucking dare," the rock says.

"I'm going to call you . . ."

"I'VE GOT A NAME!"

". . . Rocky."

Rocky stares at me. It's more of a glare, really. I start laughing again. Damn, it feels good.

"You're the worst human I've ever met," Rocky says.

I wipe the tears from my cheeks. "I think maybe when the supply shuttle comes, I'll just keep you. Not tell the labcoats about you."

"That's called kidnapping, you sadistic ape."

This makes me laugh some more. It's the accent. It kills me.

"Are you stoned?" Rocky asks.

And this is too much. I double over and clutch my shins, there in the command pod, not a stitch of clothing on, laughing and crying and wheezing for breath, fearing I might not be able to stop, that I'll die like this, die from so much joy and mirth, while debris from a destroyed cargo ship peppers the hull and cracks into the solar array, and ships full of people navigate through space at twenty times the speed of light, narrowly avoiding this great reef of drifting rocks, and all because I'm here, because I'm holding it together, this trained and hairless monkey in outer space.

CHAPTER

11

Rocky and I sit up in the business end of the beacon, past the weightless tube that extends off to the side for a dozen meters, up where the GWB broadcasts all the local gravitational disturbances to ships traveling through hyperspace. My head rests against the broadcasting dome, which makes me feel like a warm hand is cradling my skull, soothing me down to my toes.

"Tell me about your homeworld," I say to Rocky. His box is positioned so he can gaze out the main porthole with me, at the stars and the wreck of debris he miraculously survived.

There's a pause. A wistful pause.

"It's beautiful," he says. And then: "You're from Earth, right?"

"Yeah," I tell him. "Until I was ten. Then moved to Orion with my dad. Then Ajax for a few months. Then New India. I was an army brat."

"Okay, okay, I didn't ask for your entire life history," Rocky says. "Well, imagine Earth, but nothing like that."

I laugh. "Gotcha."

We sit in silence for a long while. It feels good up here. Even better with the company. I could do another four years. I could re-up. I remember feeling this way in the army, the days that were really good, when you'd survived the bad shit and felt kinda invincible and actually, deeply happy, but maybe in an unhealthy and manic kinda way, and how those were the days when you went to your CO and saluted and shouted, in your best boot camp voice, "Sign me up for another tour, SUR!" And how later, when the high wore off, and you came down from the survivor's rush, and your mood went back to normal, you were like, "What the fuck did I just do?"

I felt that kind of good right then.

After a while, Rocky starts telling me about his home planet. I listen while I gaze out at the stars and the twinkle of aluminum tinsel.

"Your race named my planet Orvo when you found it. After the name of a physician on one of the scout ships. I think he'd died the week before or something. Anyway, you probably assume that my planet and my name sound like some gibberish series of clicks and scratchy noises, and while that's really fucking xenophobic, you'd be right."

Rocky makes a series of clicks and scratchy noises. I smile. Life is really good.

"We don't have a moon, and our sun is a very long way away. What heat we have comes from a radioactive core, and there's very little tectonic activity, which makes for an incredibly still planet, covered with a few meters of water in most places, except for these really shallow ledges and flat islands where most of the cool stuff takes place. That was home."

"So, not space-faring, I assume?" I say.

"Yeah, asshole, not space-faring."

"But sentient."

"Smarter than you."

I smile. "And your anatomy? I assume something like neurons?"

"Not quite as simple as neurons, but similar. And yeah, we're very social. So we developed sentience. Theory of mind and all that."

"What's theory of mind?" I ask.

Rocky pauses. Like he's wondering if teaching a monkey is within his boundaries of patience.

"It's me being able to guess what you're thinking," he says.

My brain is already drifting to a different topic. "What do you call a small group of your kind?" I ask.

"Say what?"

"Well, a group of cows is a herd. What's a group of rocks. A bag?"

"A bag of rocks?" Rocky asks.

I laugh.

"Fuck you."

"Rocky, you're the best friend I've ever had."

"That settles it. I used to argue with the professor that there was no such thing as hell. I was wrong. I relent. I give up. I've found the joint."

"Where did you learn English?" I ask. "And who did you used to argue about heaven and hell with? This professor?"

"We didn't argue. We *debated*. We *discussed*. It's what civilized people do. You should try it sometime."

"Okay." I feel a little more sober. And for some reason, I don't mind. I sit up, away from the GWB for a moment. "Tell me about your owner—"

"I own me," Rocky says.

"Yeah, sorry." I shake my head. "About this professor you were being sent to. On Oxford."

"I'm his research assistant," Rocky says. "I just finished my internship on Delphi, was heading home. I work with Professor Bockman on human studies and consciousness."

"So you're a biologist?" I ask, and a new level of stunned hits me, followed by a wave of obviousness. Of course this thing has a job. This *being*, not thing. So many layers of biases and assumptions to peel away. Just when I think I'm almost there—

"Not a biologist," Rocky says. "I've been studying under Professor Bockman for three years. He's a philosopher."

Something clicks.

Something funny.

"Wait," I say.

"Don't—" Rocky warns.

"Are you telling me—?"

"Ah, hell," Rocky says.

"You're a philosopher's stone?"

•••

It takes a solid minute or two to stop laughing. Lying on my side, curled up in a ball, I finally get my breath back and just stay there, gazing out at the stars, feeling contentment for the first time in . . . possibly forever. I think about the passenger liner that skated through unharmed, probably safe by no more than a few seconds of desperate struggle on my part, and how no one has asked me about that. How not a single labcoat asked me how that felt. How I sat right here, exhausted and crying, but feeling something like elation, like whatever the highest form of relief in the world is, that feeling after a bomb misses its target and you've still got all your fingers and toes, but that feeling times five thousand.

"The army really fucked you up good, didn't it?" Rocky asks.

I don't answer. Instead the world goes blurry with tears.

"I'm sorry for that," Rocky tells me, and I can hear that he's sincere, and this starts the sobbing. I haven't cried in front of anyone in the longest time. Not since that one session with that army shrink, which made me never want to sit in therapy again. But now I cry my fucking guts out, and it goes on forever, and Rocky doesn't say anything, doesn't judge me, just sits in his box where I can't see him, and I know that he's smarter than me, and wiser, and it's not just the accent, but all that schooling, and that he somehow gets that I'm fucked up but that it isn't my fault, and this feels really fucking amazing, to have someone think it's not all my fault, and so I cry and cry while little pebbles and bits of steel bounce off my beacon and go tumbling like shed tears out into the cosmos.

When I finally pull it together, Rocky asks me a question, one that stuns me into a long and thoughtful silence:

"What hurt you?"

This causes me to suck in a big gulp of air. I'd cry more if I hadn't just cried myself out.

"I don't know," I say.

"Maybe you do," Rocky suggests, "but you're scared to give it life."

I laugh. "You sound like my shrink."

"Yeah, well, fuck me, maybe I'm starting to care about you a little bit, and maybe he cared about you. I mean, I'm relying on you to water me, right? And I'm really hoping to hell you tell the supply ship about me and get me home, so it behooves me to be nice to you."

"You said behooves," I say.

"Is this how you avoid thinking about it? Whatever it was?"

I sit up. I move across the space between the GWB and the outer wall of the pod and sit with my back to the porthole, looking at the dome and the smaller panes of glass that ring the small space.

"I used to be a pilot," I say.

I take a deep breath, wondering where the hell I'm going with this.

"I saw a lot of action in the Void War. We were . . . a bunch of people dying out in the middle of nowhere, you know? Not even a rock to claim. Nothing but lines on a star chart. Just pointless. Only made sense if you were drunk, you know? Like . . . how the deck of a ship seems to come to rest with a few rums, like it all balances out if you get the mixture just right, if the world is as tilted as you are."

Rocky listens. Is really listening.

"Anyway, I lost my wings and got moved to the front. I was there for the Blitz, when we were going to end the war, be home by Christmas, all that bullshit. I was in my third tour with the army. Was a lieutenant in an A-squad, which is the people you call when no one else will pick up the goddamn phone, and really, I just kept getting promoted through attrition. Everyone above me got blown to bits, and they kept slotting me up, and no one cared that my breath could strip the camo paint from a field blaster, they just cared that we killed more than we lost, which we did in spades."

My mind drifts back to that last day. My last day fighting. The day I refused to fight anymore. And my hand settles on the wound across my belly.

"I could've killed a shitload of 'em that day," I say. "I guess I already had, but I could've taken out a hive, an entire nest of hives, and turned the tide. Would've meant wiping out three of our own platoons, and I'd already lost every man in my squad, but taking the whole place out was the right thing to do. And yet I didn't. Then it turned out for the best. The Ryph pulled back because of my squad's push right up into the swarm—and yeah, it was my squad that did all the hero-ing that day, and because I'm the one who woke up in a hospital, who didn't die out there, my guts sewn back into my belly, they pinned a medal on me, and there were a bunch of parades that I saw from my hospital bed, and I still don't know why the hell anyone cared that two armies decided they'd kill each other tomorrow instead of that afternoon, and I never asked.

"My CO's CO's CO came to me with all his gold stars on his collar and asked me what I wanted to do with the rest of my career, to name my posting."

I pause and think back to that day. To that old man. His beaming face. The pride he had in the injured soldier his army had made.

"And what did you ask for?" Rocky said.

"I told him I wanted to be alone."

I remember the old man's smile fading, how the scars across his lips came back together, which let me know that he hadn't been smiling when whatever caused those scars happened to him. He walked away, but he granted me my wish.

"NASA is where the best of the best pilots end up," I tell Rocky. "The very best fliers, with all their shit together, they end up in NASA. It's always been like that. Until me."

We sit in silence a while.

"I think you're doing just fine," Rocky says. "You rescued me, right?"

I lean forward and put my face in my palms. I don't say it, but I'm thinking it, wondering who rescued whom.

It feels good, talking about this stuff. Not for the first time, I regret that I didn't continue on with the shrink. I just wasn't ready. Was too scared to face myself. It was too early to be seen.

"Hey, Rocky?"

I lift my head from my palms. Scoot over toward the box. Rocky is sitting in his little puddle, which looks about the same size as when I first made it.

"Rock?"

He looks up at me, I guess wondering what I'm about to say.

I toy with one of the splinters from his box, bending it back and forth until it comes free. Bringing it up to my nose, I breathe in the scent of wood, admire how moist and green and fresh the wood is, like it just came out of the forest, this thing that was so recently alive. It smells like my childhood on Earth. It smells like the outdoors. Like crisp air and atmosphere.

Rocky has fallen silent. I think I know why.

"You made this hole, didn't you?" I ask him.

He stares at me guiltily.

"You're like . . . like a bullet in an abdomen."

Rocky looks slightly away.

"You hurt this box, and it was still a little bit alive out there, and it was going to Professor Bockman at SAU on Oxford, and it was empty, just a box, and the wood died the rest of the way when you struck it, didn't it?"

Rocky says nothing.

"I'm losing my fucking mind, aren't I?"

I think Rocky nods. I think he does. I wish he would say something. I wish he would talk to me. But he's just a rock.

A rock with a dark line that I wish was a mouth.

A rock with spots that I wish were little blinking eyes.

My OCD roommate looks up from the sofa in my mind with this sad expression, like he knew all along, like he's the sane one.

Yeah, he's the sane one, who has to touch his tongue to one side of his mouth twenty times, and then the other side twenty times, and then the top twenty times, and this keeps the mortars away. This makes the mortars hit further down the trench. Kills someone else.

Yeah, he's the sane one.

I'm the one talking to a rock.

This is the problem with illusions: They form easy enough, but once they fall apart, they're impossible to put back together. They're like humans in that way.

Hard enough to know if a thing is alive or dead. So hard sometimes.

I smell that splinter of wood again, which still smells vaguely of the living, and I don't know why, but my mind drifts to Alice Waters, whom I loved in high school, and whom I used to write in the army because I didn't know whom else to write, and I wonder what she thought of all those batshit letters I sent, and if those letters smelled of someone who was alive and breathing and scared out of his fucking mind, or if maybe they just smelled of crazy and desperate and blood and thermite. Or if, like me, those old love letters just reeked to her of war.

BOUNTY

CHAPTER

12

They say bad things come in threes, but I don't think that's true. I think bad things keep right on coming. They don't stop. They'll never stop. It's just too depressing to keep counting, so we start over after the third bad thing. We hold our breath. We wait. We hope the universe will wait with us.

But then something else bad happens, and with dread and short memories we utter to ourselves, "Okay, that's one," and we brace for what's next.

Something's always next.

I live in a tin can on the edge of sector eight, and my job is to keep bad things from happening. My track record so far is less than stellar. A screensaver on one of my monitors reads *18 Days Since Our Last Accident*. It ticks up by one each morning, so that's progress.

Most ships pass through my sector at twenty times the speed of light, and they leave little more than a ripple on my grav scanner. But near on three weeks ago, some bastards took down my beacon, and a cargo bound for Vega splashed itself across the asteroid field in my back yard. Most of the wreck is still out there—what the pirates and scavengers and souvenir seekers didn't cart off.

I guess if we're counting, that was the first bad thing. The second was a little incident I'd rather not mention, but it involved a talking rock. Okay, it involved me talking to a rock—I'm pretty sure the rock never talked back. Just in case, I drilled a hole straight through the guy and hung him around my neck on a lanyard. Not sure if I did this to make sure the rock was really dead or to keep him close to my ears in case he talks again. Told you I wasn't proud.

The third thing is the reason my body is covered in bruises, cuts, and scrapes right now. It's why my ankle is either sprained or broken and my arm is in a sling. Two days ago, my grav panels started oscillating uncontrollably. Really turns a man's world upside down. And right-side up again. And upside down. And—well, you get the point.

Now I'm a mess and my beacon's a mess. Tools, food packs, spares, all went rattling around in their cubbies and cabinets until they burst forth like possessed demons. Hundreds of items are scattered all over the place, choosing to lie perfectly still now, like they're all exhausted from the pounding they gave me. Taking naps. Waiting for me to tuck them all back in.

Before I do that, I'm wiring up kill switches for the grav generator. I put big red buttons on the ceilings of every living module and run wires to breakers down in life support. Can't step on the buttons by accident, but if my tin can gives me the old shake-and-bake again, I can hit one of these instead of trying to get down a ladder while gravity is rag-dolling me. Trying to get down the ladder the last time was what took my arm out of its socket.

I could probably call the incident in and list my wounds, and it'd be enough for NASA to send me home. Problem is, I don't have a home to go to. Some part of me knows I'm here for life. And the way things are going, I reckon that won't be for very long.

I finish the last wire splice on the new kill switches. Even with the floor grates up for access, I have to wiggle back under some of the pipes and conduits to reach the grav generator. Wrapping electrical tape around the splice, I laugh to see the same tape wrapped around one of my fingers. I ran out of bandages, so I resorted to taping up my cuts. The same stuff holds us together, me and my beacon. Hell, most of this place is a modification some previous operator made. It's like a human body at age thirty-five, when not a single original cell is left. All that remains are the memories—the one damn thing we wish we could amputate.

Funny how that works. And funny how easily we forget the good times while the nightmares haunt us. Guess that's a survival mechanism. We're not here to be happy; we're just here to be here. I spend a lot of time wishing I wasn't— but that's my dark secret, and not something I'm going to tell you. I don't even whisper that to my rock.

Three bad things. They come like this, in little clusters for the counting. They're coming for me now.

Ding-Dong.

The first of them arrives with the sound of a door chime.

•••

Okay, it's not quite a door chime; it's actually a hull proximity alert. But if you ask me, the old alert sounded too much like an air raid siren. Which ain't so bad when it's occasional, but with all the traffic after the cargo crash, it started jangling my nerves. It's the waiting for it to go off that kills me. It's the silent anticipation. Your whole body is tense, lying awake in your sleep sack, eyes wide open, seeing a buddy yell *INCOMING!* before a cloud of red mist blooms where a human once stood. Yeah, it's not the sound of the siren that gets you. It's the lying there, waiting. Listening to the silence. Counting.

I did some digging, figured out where the sound file for the alert was stored, and replaced it with a door chime. Of course, I couldn't find a door chime in the archives, so I had to record my own. And yeah, I could've made a decent chiming sound with a wrench and some sheet steel, but I got lazy and just said *Ding-Dong* into the mic. Now, when I get a visitor, that's what I hear. Gives me a chuckle. Sometimes, you've just gotta laugh. You just gotta hug your shins, rock back and forth, and laugh.

I wiggle my way out of the crawlspace, scooting along on my shoulder blades, rolling from one to the other, and pushing with my good foot.

Ding-Dong.

That's me.

Ding-Dong.

I'm coming.

I pull myself out of the crawlspace and limp my way through the scattered debris. The climb up the ladder is slow with one hand and a sprained ankle. In the living quarters, I silence the alert using the switch by my sleep sack, then go up another flight into the command module. There's a blast of static from the high frequency radio before a voice cuts in with a transmission.

"—con 23, this is Sanity's Edge, over."

I lift the mic with my free hand and wince as a stab of pain shoots across my ribs. Glancing out the nearest porthole, I see a ship hovering three or four klicks away, red and green lights blinking on each wingtip. Long pods with glimmering gold tips hang beneath the wings. Lasers. Pointing at me.

"Beacon 23," I say. "Go ahead, Sanity."

Checking the scanners, I see she's registered to a Delphi corporation. The Delphi system is a tax-free zone; a lot of privately owned vessels hail from there, even if they've never touched atmo in Delphi. They just do the bill of sale in orbit and scoot.

"Permission to dock," the pilot radios. "Official US marshal business."

I glance back out the porthole. That ain't no marshal boat out there. If she's privately owned, and she's really on marshal business, and she's legally armed, then it can only be one thing: a bounty hunter. Looks like a whiff of excitement has drifted into old sector eight. I squeeze the mic.

"Beacons are NASA-oversight neutral territory," I remind the captain. "By colregs, no arms are allowed on any beacon, nor are military or private security craft allowed to dock without warrant or express permission."

Which is true and all, but what I'm really thinking is that the beacon's a wreck, as am I, and I really don't want visitors. I'm in my white NASA boxer briefs, and putting on a shirt with a bad shoulder is a pain in the ass. Well, not the ass, exactly, but you know what I mean.

"Beaming the warrant to you now," the radio hisses.

I check my comm screen as the transmission comes through. After a brief scan, my systems tell me the document's legit. There's a twinge in my ribs as I take a deep breath.

"Docking collar Charlie," I say. I reach over and flip on the homing light and energize the locking collar. Then I think of a little white lie. "Uh . . . Captain, I'm under strict quarantine, so please stay aboard. I'll come to you."

There's a pause on the other side.

"Quarantine?" the pilot asks.

"No longer communicable," I assure him—and I feel like I can hear him exhale in relief.

If he checks the colreg logs, he'll see that I'm not exactly lying. I *am* under quarantine. What the logs won't say is that it was a computer virus, and that the victim was my beacon. Strange the lengths I'll go to in order to keep people away from me, considering how lonely I feel most of the time. I guess that's the strange torment I suffer: dying for company, for someone to talk to, but it's never the right someone who shows. And an unwelcome presence is far worse than miserable silence.

•••

I head down three sets of ladders to the lock hub, the sling over my arm making the trip take longer than usual. Any weight on the ball of my left foot makes my ankle cry out, so I try to get my heel deep on the rungs, which just means repeatedly banging my shin. I considered going without gravity for a while, but one look at all the crap strewn everywhere and I imagine it floating and bouncing around. No thanks.

In fact, the wreck of my beacon comes into stark relief with the prospect of someone docking up. In addition to the stuff everywhere, I've got open access panels leading down into mechanical spaces and wires strung all over from my makeshift repairs. My walk suit is crumpled up in the middle of the docking module, and the door to the lifeboat is wide open. For a while there, I was wearing the suit all the time and sleeping in the lifeboat, but I stopped doing both those things after the shipwreck debris bombarding my beacon died down. Besides, I'm back to not sleeping much anyway.

I wait by the airlock for the pilot to secure his ship. Sniffing the air, I have this bad feeling that, despite the herculean effort from the air scrubbers and NASA's PineFresh scenting system, the entire facility reeks of a college dorm room, midsummer, after an egg fight, with two dead skunks under a pile of soiled laundry. I breathe into my palm and sniff. Whatever olfactory sense I had died months ago. That's good for me, bad for visitors.

A loud thump against the hull lets me know that the ship has arrived and that the pilot is a three on a scale of ten when it comes to jockeying a flight stick. If he's making a living collecting bounties, that probably means he's more of a terrestrial threat. More of a sleuth-and-taser kinda guy. This guess is vindicated once I've keyed my side of the airlock and he's keyed his. The bounty hunter on the other side is straight out of one of those true-life holos where people repo your shit or haul you back to jail from some remote moon hideout.

His hair is in dreadlocks. His beard is long, and it's knotted with bits of string so that it juts out in little clumps. There's an unlit cigar between his teeth and mirrored shades wrapping his face. He's got a bandana around his neck, another on his bicep, and one tied around each knee. His flightsuit is studded with bulging pockets, and even standing perfectly still, he jangles. I imagine he must keep the grav on his ship at a 0.7 to be able to stand all that nonsense. He has guns strapped everywhere, and an honest-to-goodness bandolier of large brass shells and grenades is draped across his chest like some warlord beauty contestant sash. What sounds vaguely like a dog yips somewhere from within the depths of his ship.

"Mitch," the bounty hunter says, reaching out his hand with a jangle and clatter. "Mitch O'Shea." We do that awkward arm-in-sling handshake where I extend my left hand, turn it sideways, and we go pinkie-to-thumb. He looks me up and down. "What happened to you?"

I realize I'm standing there in my boxers, barefoot, covered in bruises and duct tape. I dimly care.

"Gravity genset went on the fritz," I say. "Started oscillating. Uncontrollably."

The bounty hunter lowers his shades and narrows his eyes at me, almost like he has some truth-detecting superpower and is boring it into my brain. I glance up at the ceiling, and he glances with me. I glance down at the floor, and he does the same. We look up again. Then down.

"Yeah," I say. "About like that."

"No shit?"

I point to my slinged arm. "You ever hear it hurts worse to put a shoulder back in than it does to knock it out?"

He nods.

"Complete crap. Feels so good going back in. Like popping your knuckles. You should try it."

"I'll take your word for it." He glances at my arm, at my attire, and then pushes his glasses back over his eyes. When he fishes a tablet from a pouch in the back of his flightsuit, I see that the small talk is over. Down to business. He holds the tablet out to me; it has a warrant displayed on the screen. I study a blurry image of a woman with short-cropped hair and an angry scowl. There's all kinds of small text about what the government wants done with her and how much they'll pay, but I just see the image. The tablet is taken back before I'm ready to let go of it.

"Have you seen her?" O'Shea asks.

"Nope," I say.

"You sure?" he asks.

"Positive."

O'Shea lowers his glasses and narrows his eyes at me again. I widen mine on purpose, throwing the blinds open, letting him really stare inside. Somewhere in his ship, an animal whimpers. If this guy could really see my thoughts, he'd probably be whimpering too.

The glasses go back up. I fight the urge to laugh out loud at this guy. There's a chance, I realize, that all his gear came from a surplus store and he's really new at this. Impossible to tell. In the army, rookies spent a lot of time charring their gear over trench fires and smearing their helmets with mud to fit in. The vets, meanwhile, spent their time trying to keep their shit maintained in order to stay alive. I sniff the air, looking for a scent of gun oil or WD-60 to get a handle on which sort of person Mitch O'Shea is. Unfortunately, due to the nature of my living quarters, my olfactory sense is stunted.

"Okay, well, I'll need all ship scans for the last couple weeks," O'Shea says. "Plus all radio logs."

"Not many places to hide out here," I say.

Mitch stares at me. At least, I assume he's staring at me behind those glasses.

"There's good reason to suspect this fugitive came through here," he says. "I'll also need to do some scans of my own, poke around a bit, but I want to warn you that this person is very dangerous—"

I say, "*Ding-Dong*," cutting O'Shea off.

Well, a recording of my voice from two weeks ago does that. There's another ship arriving in-system. I glance up the ladders, dreading the three-flight climb. It's fifty-six rungs to the command level. Yes, I've been counting.

"Was that someone saying 'ding-dong'?" O'Shea asks. He points his unlit cigar at the ceiling.

I clear my throat. Beacons aren't meant for co-habitating. It feels like the NASA techs just left, and now I've got this guy seeing me in my briefs, nosing my dirty laundry, and hearing what I do to pass the time.

"You mind if I look out your canopy?" I ask. "Just to see who that is. It's a long climb up with a busted wing." I indicate the sling.

Mitch hesitates. Then he stands aside with a jingle and a jangle. "Don't touch anything," he says. "Cockpit's this way."

Yeah, toward the front of the ship, I nearly say sarcastically. From the bump he gave the locking collar, I'm pretty sure I've got more flight time than this bounty hunter does. But I keep it to myself and follow him toward the cockpit. We pass through what looks like a holding pen—gray bars run from floor to ceiling. There's an animal in one of the pens, drinking out of a toilet.

"Cricket, stop that. No. Bad girl."

The animal pulls its head out and turns to look at its master, water dribbling from its jowls. Looks like a cross between a dog and a leopard. Probably not even a little bit of either. Definitely alien. The animal goes back to slurping.

"Hardened criminal?" I ask, jabbing my thumb at the cell.

O'Shea laughs. "Cricket? Naw, I just put her away so she don't maul you."

I look back at the animal. She's the size of the cougars we'd see now and then in the backwoods of Tennessee.

Might be deadly, but I doubt it. Seems like a pushover, drinking out of that toilet and looking at us with that blank expression.

I follow O'Shea through a narrow hall. There's an open door to a bunkroom with an unmade bed; just beyond that are some grated lockers with guns inside and big padlocks on the latches. We squeeze past these into the tight cockpit, and O'Shea pulls up his system scanner. I peer out the porthole to see another dark-hulled ship approaching the beacon.

"Goddamn," O'Shea says.

"You got an ID on that?" I ask. The ship looks vaguely military. I don't like things that look vaguely military. I hate the things that look *really* military. With me, it's like a sliding scale of hate versus appearance with some direct correlation.

"Don't need an ID," he says, disgust dripping from his voice. He reaches across me for the HF mic. Squeezing the transmit button, he glares plasma rounds up through the canopy. "You know putting hull trackers on a bounty ship is a federal violation, right, asshole?"

The radio hisses a response: *"You think I need a hull tracker to sniff you down, you filthy runt of a raped pig?"*

I'm beginning to suspect these two know each other. I watch this new ship expel little volcano blasts of air as it orients itself to face us.

"He's not going to shoot us, is he?" I ask.

"Nah, Vlad here is a *chickenshit.*"

I notice O'Shea squeezes the mic and raises his voice as he says this last bit.

"What did he mean by a 'raped pig'?" I ask.

O'Shea shrugs. "He's not so bright. Stay away from him."

I look Mitch O'Shea up and down and consider what it might mean for this guy to label someone else "not bright." Thoughts of black holes come to mind.

The HF squawks again. I adjust the squelch, since Mitch doesn't seem to care to. Or maybe doesn't know how. *"Beacon 23, this is Vladimir Bostokov on federal marshal duty. Requesting docking procedures. I have a warrant. Over."*

"Fuck him," Mitch says, with all the disgust of a man with a shitload of debt who feels very close to a large pile of credits and sees another man eyeing that same pile.

"I've got to let him," I say, waving Mitch for the mic.

"You could claim a section 12b, extenuating circumstances related to injury in the line of duty." He nods at my sling, all the bandages over my little cuts and scrapes, and the array of purple splotches.

"*Now* you tell me," I say. I key the mic to radio this Vlad character. "This is the operator of beacon 23. Locking collar Bravo. I'm under quarantine, so please stay aboard. Over."

"Copy," Vlad says.

And beside me, Mitch O'Shea rattles in annoyance.

CHAPTER 13

"Look, I don't really want *either* of you on my beacon," I tell O'Shea as we wait by airlock Bravo. "You've both got warrants for scans, so you'll both get them. Then you'll get the hell off my station."

"I'm telling you, this guy's an asshole," O'Shea warns.

The light above the airlock goes green, signaling the second bounty hunter's ship has a good magnetic seal and that the atmo on the other side is clean. I didn't even hear the hull make contact, the landing was so soft. I glance at O'Shea, but he's fuming and oblivious. Vlad might be an asshole, I want to say, but he's a damn good pilot.

I key open the airlock. A bewildering sight awaits. There's a man in a tuxedo on the other side of the door.

"Vladimir Morrow Bostokov," the man says, extending his hand to me.

I accept his hand with my inverted left. Before I can introduce myself, Vlad shoots his colleague a nasty look. "Mitchell," he says, in his thick accent.

O'Shea says nothing in return.

Vlad reaches inside his jacket pocket and pulls out a printed sheet of paper. He unfolds it, and I can see it's the same bounty O'Shea showed me.

"What do to your arm?" Vlad says, leaving out a non-vital word in there somewhere.

"Grav panel issues," I say. He looks me up and down in my boxers and bandages, seems to be waiting for more than this. "Fluctuations," I tell him. "Polarity issues. Went for a bounce or two."

Vlad shrugs. I gesture toward the printed flyer. "And no, I've never seen her."

"Here," Vlad says, handing me the flyer anyway. "Keep for you."

Perhaps too eagerly, I accept the flyer and fold it back up, sticking it in the waistband of my boxers.

"*Ding-Dong*," I hear myself say.

"What now?" I ask.

The two bounty hunters stare at one another.

"You mind?" I point into Vlad's ship. He shrugs, and I step past him and enter what looks more like a swanky hotel than a star cruiser. Everything is large clean slabs in that pre-post-second-modern style. Some black and white photos hang on the walls, mostly alien portraits either staring right at the camera or off to the side. They almost look like mug shots, but artfully done. A wet bar in one corner gleams with shiny bottles of all shapes, most of them half-full of a myriad shades of amber.

Vlad waves me forward, leading us past transparent doors that look in on small posh rooms. In one of these rooms, a young man looks up from a bunk, his hands shackled in iron fists. I realize these rooms are cells. I'd kill to live in one. They look amazing.

Behind us, I hear O'Shea jangling and following along. He grumbles enviously about something or other. Vlad tells him to not touch that.

I duck my head and enter a meticulously kept cockpit. You can smell the leather. The place is so nice that even my nose is perking up. O'Shea and Vlad crowd in beside me, and all three of us peer out the canopy.

"I don't like this," O'Shea says.

"Me either," says Vlad.

In the distance, my voice whispers, "*Ding-Dong*."

"Look, it's not my favorite day this week," I tell the two bounty hunters. "And yesterday, I cleaned the shitter."

It takes me a moment to find the new arrival, to see what the bounty hunters are seeing. This third ship is matte black. It can be picked out only by the background stars it gobbles and shits out as it moves across the constellations. A dim red and green light glows at each wingtip, but probably below legal illumination levels. A white light flashes from the nose of the ship, directed toward my beacon. Pulses of long and short.

I locate the HF on Vlad's dash and pick up the mic without asking. Legally, with the ships docked to my beacon, they're under my command. Warrant or no.

"Won't need that," O'Shea says, squinting up at the ship.

I ignore him and squeeze the mic. "Vessel inbound at beacon 23, state your intentions."

"Won't work," Vlad says. "She no talk."

"Who is that?" I ask the two bounty hunters, who both seem to know something about this ship. "Another friend of yours?"

"I've crossed paths with her once or twice," O'Shea says. And I note the lack of ire in his voice. Maybe even something like respect. "Don't know her name, but she makes the quiet type sound like an afterbooster in atmo."

"Well, surely she listens," I say. I watch the flashes. My Morse is rusty, but the context helps; I get the marshal business bit of her spiel.

"Well, looks like she wants to board. Seeing as I've only got the three lock collars, and my lifeboat ain't moving, you two should clear out. I'll beam all the scans and logs I have to the lot of you, and to anyone else who shows up."

Vlad shrugs. He seems to be okay with this. O'Shea grimaces at me. As we pass back through the ship, O'Shea pulls me aside. He's holding a few bills of Federation money out to me. "Give me a thirty-minute head start," he whispers.

I turn to study him. He adds: "For getting here first. And saving you a trip to your radio."

I take the money and pocket it. O'Shea smiles. The boy in the cell is watching us through his long black bangs, but he returns his gaze to the floor when I glare at him. We follow Vlad back to the beacon, where the two colleagues exchange thin frowns and disappear into their respective ships. Using the keypads by the doors, I close the airlocks on both of them.

•••

After the two bounty hunters decouple and pull away, I watch through the porthole as the black hull of the third craft comes into view. There's no seeing inside it, as its canopy and all its portholes are tinted. The ship quickly fills my porthole, and the pilot docks with a very capable nine on the bump-o-meter. I wait for the light to go green, key open the airlock, and find a ninja standing on the other side.

A bit of a derail here to say what a huge fan I was of *Urban Ninja Detroit* growing up. All I ever wanted to be was an urban ninja. My parents got me a costume for Halloween when I was seven or eight, and I kept wearing that getup until the split-toe shoes would barely squeeze onto my feet and the pants rode up above my calves. Because of me, everything in my neighborhood was peppered with holes from throwing stars and blowdarts. Hell, I probably joined the military instead of going to college because of the overdeveloped sense of honor that damn TV show gave me. I'll also say here that I like to pretend *Urban Ninja L.A.* never existed. *Urban Ninja Chicago* wasn't so bad. But I digress.

"Lemme guess," I say to the ninja. "Looking for a certain fugitive?"

The bounty hunter, who is dressed from head to toe in all black, with cowl and goggles and everything, nods. I see that most of the black attire is a mix and match of official navy reg gear. I recognize much of it, and even know the decade some of it was in service and the field of action in which it was assigned. Someone hit up the surplus store and found a sale.

"Haven't seen her," I say.

The bounty hunter pulls out a small tablet and keys something in, I assume to show me the text or to make the tablet speak out loud. I'm sensing that this person *can't* speak, rather than that she chooses not to.

"You want the scans," I say.

She nods and wipes the screen with the side of her hand. Starts writing something else.

"And radio logs."

Another nod. And I think I can tell from the movement of shadows across her cowled cheeks that she's smiling.

"No problem," I say. "I've got a quarantine situation here from NASA, so you've got to stay on your ship. I'll beam you the data. You need anything else?"

For some reason, I've always felt the urge to go out of my way for those who ask for the *least*, rather than those who ask the loudest. But she shakes her head.

"Okay. If you'll pull away, I'll go up and get you and your two buddies what you need." I say this, even though I kinda don't want her to go. But I'm embarrassed about how I look and how the beacon looks. My life is all about miserable timing.

Instead of turning back to her ship, the bounty hunter hesitates, like there's something else.

I hazard a guess: "You want a head start, don't you?"

She nods.

I think of all those mornings sitting in front of my TV watching masterless warriors scale glass towers and fight back the hordes of shoguns sent by the evil Tao-

Lin Corporation. I have a soft spot for ladies in all black. Probably the real reason I joined the navy.

"You've got it," I say, my free hand dropping to my waistband, where the bills from O'Shea peek out next to a folded bounty flyer. "Good luck on your hunt."

I don't really mean this last. In fact, I feel rather conflicted as the bounty hunter disappears and I work my slow way up the first ladder. It feels like the grav panels have gone on the fritz again, twisting me this way and that. Sometimes you want the good guys to get their man. Sometimes you can't tell who the good guys are.

Up the second ladder, into my living quarters, I silence the proximity alarm again. Then I head up the last ladder into the command pod, and my mind goes back to how bad things seem to come in threes. Three bounty hunters, arriving within moments of each other. Can I count them as three individual bad things and assume my day improves? I decide to.

A voice interrupts my thoughts.

"Those assholes gone?" someone says.

I emerge up the ladder and turn to see a woman sitting in my command chair. She's got a blaster in her hand and a frown splashed across her face.

It's the girl from the bounty flyer.

I never thought I'd see her again.

CHAPTER 14

"Jesus, Scarlett, what the hell are you doing here?"

"Are they gone?"

"Yes, they're gone. They're out there looking for you. What're you doing here?"

I take a step toward her, and the blaster stiffens in her hand. She looks me up and down and smirks at my attire. The wounds across my body don't seem to faze her. She's seen me in worse condition than this. And in fewer clothes.

"What am I doing here?" she asks. "Don't be dense. I came to find you."

"Why? How? And you do realize you brought the badass brigade with you, right?" I nod toward the portholes. Scarlett doesn't glance away from me. Instead, she shrugs.

"I needed a ride," she says.

That's when it hits me how she got here. She must've stowed away on one of their ships, then probably tipped them off that she was here. I reckon she had to've been on one of the first two ships, and got out when we were in

Vlad's cockpit. I'd wager O'Shea brought her here. Vlad's ship was too neat for hiding.

"Nice blaster," I say, gesturing with my free hand. "I thought we were friends."

I should mention here that I really don't like guns pointed at my head. Not unless I'm the one doing the pointing.

"So you're working for NASA," Scarlett says, as if this answers my question. "Why?"

I let out a sigh. Scarlett never could stand any government agency. Doesn't matter what they do, they aren't to be trusted.

"I needed a job," I say.

"Tell me why you're working for NASA," Scarlett insists.

"Money," I say. "Pension. Job. Dinero."

She raises the blaster. Her voice as well. "Why are you working for NASA?"

I scratch one of the bandages on my arm. They say the itch is a sign of healing. I've been healing for a long damn time.

"I needed to be alone," I whisper.

The blaster wavers. I try to remember the last time I saw Scarlett. In a trench on Gturn, I think. Or one of its moons. A lot of those trenches looked the same.

The blaster lowers a little. She believes me. She should. I told her the truth. I always do, eventually.

"Now please tell me what *you're* doing here," I say. "How'd you find me?"

Scarlett points the blaster toward one of the portholes. I turn to see the sparkle of debris out there like a billion new stars. And it makes sense. Sometimes bad things really do come in clusters, because one leads to the other. I think about the rock, which I wouldn't have found were it not for the wreck. I think about the wreck I am, which Scarlett wouldn't have found without the accident.

"NASA has to file a report with the navy when there's a wreck like that," she says. "We've been looking for you for a long time. Your name finally popped up."

"Yeah, well, I've been looking to not be found." I turn back to her. "Can you put the blaster away? Please? I'm not a government stooge."

"If you're working for their pension, you're their stooge."

She says this, but the blaster goes away, back in her holster. In the porthole behind her, I see the flashing lights from one of the ships. "Shit," I say. "I've got to transmit some stuff."

The blaster comes right back out, but I ignore her. She isn't here to shoot me. I start a wireless handshake with the three ships and then begin transmitting the scan logs and radio exchanges to the black ship first. I put in a five-minute delay to transmit to O'Shea, and a twenty-minute delay for Vlad. I message Vlad privately and warn him of bandwidth issues. Scarlett watches me the entire time. The procedure takes me longer than usual using one hand. Only now does she show some concern for my physical state.

"Still beating yourself up, huh?"

"Ha," I say. "Grav panel issues."

She snorts like she doesn't believe me. I fish the bounty flyer out of my waistband and hold it out it to her. "Fifty million creds," I point out.

Scarlett laughs and waves it away. "I got a copy. And I'm worth more than that. *You're* worth more than that."

"I don't want any part of this."

"You think you get to choose?" Scarlett laughs. And now I can't remember if I liked her or hated her back in the day. It was my first tour on the ground. I've blocked a lot of that out.

She laughs some more and shakes her head. "You don't want any part of this. Tell your parents that. The day they screwed in the back seat of some car in Kentucky, they put you here. Right here." She aims the blaster at the floor, like she's indicating the beacon.

I watch as one of the ships outside peels away toward the asteroid field.

"Tennessee," I say, correcting her.

"Whatever."

"Yeah, well, I think I do have a choice. I came out here to get away from the war—"

"News flash," Scarlett says, cutting me off. "The war's coming to you, Bub. You're on the front lines."

"This is *not* the front lines," I say. She knows this isn't the front lines. I don't care what my dreams tell me, what the shakes mean, the things I see and hear when I'm alone. The war isn't here. It can't be. This is a different war on my beacon, between just me and my demons.

"Every square inch of this galaxy is a front line," Scarlett says. "It's just a matter of when. But it doesn't have to be like that—"

Not this. I think I remember now that I mostly didn't

like Scarlett. It's the narrow eyes. The way they think they see something that isn't there. Conspiratorial eyes. But she stands up and moves like a cat across the module and stands close enough to me that I can smell how clean she is, this little pocket of freshness in the dank and dark, and I want to kiss her. I want to grab something beautiful and hold it and weep and smother it with affection so that maybe it won't ever leave me. And that's when I remember that I didn't like Scarlett Mulhenry at all. And I didn't hate her either. I think I loved her.

"Why are you here?" I ask, and I feel like I have to shout it, but it comes out a whisper, like my nightmare voice.

"I want you to end this war," Scarlett says.

Her eyes widen for a moment.

I can see in them.

I can see that she's dead serious.

15
CHAPTER

I remember kids who thought they could end wars. Hell, I remember *being* one of those kids. Neighborhoods have always been full of them, running around with plastic blasters and blowing the heads off Ryph, pretending we're shooting the last shot in the war, bringing it all to a heroic end. When we're young, every imaginary battle ends with heroics. Finales come with a bang. Then you get older, and you see that life ends in wrinkles and whimpers.

Looking at Scarlett now, as she looks at me, and her ridiculous words about ending wars hang in the air, I remember more than just the fact that I loved her once; I almost remember what it *felt* like. I almost feel it again. Love comes as fast as shrapnel in the trenches. It's indiscriminate. It gets whoever's closest. When it's your time, it's your time. They assign someone to the bunk beside you, and it's like a grenade landing in your lap.

I vaguely remember what I felt like before the war took my hope, and I vaguely remember what Scarlett was like before the war did something screwy with hers.

"I don't have room for your dreams," I tell her. "You shouldn't have come here. I don't know how we'll get you out, but I'll help you do that. It's a capital offense, but I'll help you. Maybe the next trader—"

"I'm not leaving here without you," she says. "A friend will come for me. For us both. Someone you know—"

I wave her silent and take a step back, like she really is a bomb that might go off. "Scarlett, I can't leave here." And then I say what I've known for a while but haven't told anyone at NASA, haven't even admitted to myself, not out loud. "I'm never leaving here," I say. "It's a two-year, but I'll re-up. This is like the army, except I'll last longer. This is where I belong."

She looks me up and down. Frowns. Her eyes glisten. "This isn't you," she says.

"It is," I tell her. And I nearly tell her my secret. My dark one. She always got the truth out of me in the past, but never without a fight. I change the subject in a hurry. Any kind of crazy is better than my kind. "So how do you think you can end this war?"

Scarlett adjusts the small pack slung over her shoulder. She pulls out a weathered paperback. Holds it up so I can see the cover.

"You've read this?" she asks.

The book is *Salaman's Battle*. It's part of the *Frontier Saga* by T.W. Rudolf. Of course I've read it. It's trench pulp, and practically required reading for grunts. We passed these novels around like VD. I read the entire series until the pages turned to mud and the spines fell apart.

"Sure," I say. I smile. "Are we going to take out the Lord hive with a planet buster like Corporal Charlie Sikes does in book twelve?" I say this with the lilt and enthusiasm of a twelve-year-old planning the next stage of the neighborhood invasion from behind Mrs. Wilkerson's petunias.

"How much do you know about Rudolf?" Scarlett asks, clearly not amused.

I shrug my one good shoulder. "I probably scanned the back of a book or two." Even before she turns the tattered paperback around, I can already see T.W.'s bald head, the fatigues he's always wearing, and that angry I-served-in-the-military-so-buy-my-book-I've-seen-the-real-shit scowl.

"There's no such person," Scarlett says. "He's as much a fiction as his stories."

I raise my hand like I'm in class. "So we expose the conspiracy, and the war ends!"

"The person behind T.W. Rudolf is a former marine intelligence officer named Porter Mencius. Porter was the numero uno translator for the armed forces during the Orion Offensive."

"I'm still not getting it—"

"These are repurposed Ryph novels, is what I'm trying to tell you."

This takes my brain a few moments. Scarlett waits patiently.

"Bullshit," I say, when I realize what she's suggesting. "You're saying someone translated Ryph novels, and that's what we've been reading? But we kick the Ryph's asses in those books. In the end, I mean. Right after it looks hopeless and all."

Scarlett does a dogfighting maneuver in the air, twisting one hand after the book. "They switch everything around," she says. "We become them. They become us." Now the book is chasing her hand. "He changed a few other details, of course. What happened is, Porter fell in love with the original stories in translation, even fell for the Ryph a little, and he figured he could make a quick buck. What were the Ryph going to do, sue him? They were already trying to kill us all. He just had to change the names and which side was which."

I think back on some of those books, many of which I read half a dozen times. Something is trying to fit together in my mind when Scarlett gives me a nudge.

"Don't you see? *We're* the alien horde."

She gives me a moment to let this sink in. It doesn't quite.

"When someone told me who the author was, and where these books came from, I went and checked a few other races we've made contact with. The Hoko, the Tryndians, the Capricorns. Guess what? They all have a long and rich popular culture dealing with alien invasions. Every one of them. And it all starts about the time each race put something into orbit for the first time."

"Okay," I say, seeing this point at least. "That makes sense. We're all scared shitless out here. It's a scary place."

"It's worse than that. Don't you see? We fear what we know we'll become. As soon as we can go out, we start worrying about something heading our way. To the Ryph, we're everything they thought we'd be. And we think the same of them."

"But they are. Look at what happened on Delphi."

"And *they* say look what happened on Arcturus. And we say Delphi happened first. And they say Arcturus was worse. And both sides are run by fear. You know why?"

I nod. "Sure. Because fear is how you hedge your bets. If you're wrong, you wiped out some friendlies. Oops. But if you're right, you saved your ass and all of humanity's."

"No, that's not why. It's because fear sells. It's because war is sport. And it's also very good business. We warred with ourselves until we found someone to war with together."

"Well, there you go," I say, snapping my fingers. "There's no stopping it. So why try? Look at me—" I wave my arm at the beacon. "I'm the hero because I checked out."

"That's exactly right," Scarlett says. "The problem is, you didn't take the rest of us with you."

•••

I have no idea what Scarlett means by this, but all the crazy talk has me thirsty. Or I just want something to occupy my free hand. I cross to the small sink by the lounge and pour Scarlett a water, then I drink from the tap. I hand her a food pack as well. I don't have any appetite, but I grab one for myself. Tearing the pack open with my teeth, I squeeze some of the protein paste into my mouth. It tastes better heated up, but the army taught me not to care.

"Tell me what you remember from that last day," Scarlett says. I notice she's eyeing the nasty knot of scars that peeks out from under my slinged arm. I haven't seen her or talked to her in years. She shouldn't know a damn thing about that day. Then I remember she tracked me here by hacking navy files. She knows the same bullshit story they know.

"More than I care to," I tell her, chewing the paste and fighting to swallow.

"I want to hear about it. And not what's in the reports. Tell me what really happened."

I turn away from her, finish the paste, and throw the packet in the recycler. Staring out the porthole, I can see one of the ships moving through the asteroid belt. There's the second ship. No sign of the ninja, which makes me smile.

"We pushed into the hive on Yata. Our platoon was pinned down. As was Echo company. Everyone in my squad ate it. That left me in charge. I was going to set off the nuke, wipe out the whole hive—"

I stop right there. I've never told this next part to anyone. Why do I do this for her?

"What happened?" she asks.

I stare out the porthole.

Scarlett takes a step toward me. I can hear her picking her way carefully through the debris scattered everywhere. She was always good at this, picking through the debris. When her hand lands on my good shoulder, I flinch, which feels like a knife slipping between my ribs.

"I know what happened," she whispers. "I just want you to admit it."

I look down at the floor. My eyes are watering. I blink that shit away.

"I didn't do it," I say. "My finger was on the button, but I didn't do it. Couldn't do it."

"You didn't set off the bomb," she says. "And next thing you know, a Ryph Lord is standing over you."

I nod. My voice would crack if I tried to use it. I feel my hand trembling. Scarlett's hand is still resting on my shoulder, burning me there.

"And he opened you up," she says. Her hand drifts down my bruised ribs and touches my stomach. My scars. I haven't been touched in so long. I'd forgotten what it feels like. I nod.

"And then you killed him, and their entire army fled the battlefield, and you saved the day."

"Yes," I whisper, lying through my teeth, pretending my account of things was how they really were.

"But you didn't kill him, did you?"

I shake my head. Tears roll down my cheeks.

"You didn't do shit."

I nod. I can feel her breasts pressing against my back.

"Why didn't you set off that bomb?" she asks me.

I don't say anything. I just concentrate on her hand. I place mine on the back of hers, holding it there.

"Because of the company you would've lost?" she asks.

"No," I whisper.

"Why, then?"

I can't say.

"Tell me. C'mon, soldier, just spit it out. I know it's right there. The truth is on the tip of your tongue."

I don't want to say.

"Tell me why you didn't do it," she commands.

And my will shatters. Maybe because of her touch. So I tell her the truth.

"Because of the hive," I whisper, barely loud enough for anyone to hear. "I couldn't do it because of the hive."

CHAPTER 16

The radio squawks. I can't tell how long we've been standing there, in a fog of my admission, her arm wrapped around me, her hand on my flesh, my hand pressed against hers. Felt like forever. Wasn't long enough.

"Son of a raped pig, do you read?"

"Fuck off, Vladimir."

I turn to look at Scarlett, who has pulled away from me at this intrusion by the HF.

"It's two of the bounty hunters," I say.

"No shit," she says.

"How many cats you have in bag right now?" Vlad asks.

"Speak English," O'Shea radios back.

"Bounties. How many in ship? I find it hard to believe you make two bounty like this, but I'm going through ship scans, and I see three warm on ship of yours, and I

·115·

know you have no friends, no girlfriend. So how you get so lucky, boy of bacon?"

"That's Vladimir," I say. "Eastern European, I think."

"I know who he is," Scarlett says.

"I don't know what you're talking about, asshole. What bounties? It's just me and my warthen, Cricket, on this ship."

There's a pause in the communications. My brain goes to where Vlad's brain is going. Three signatures on O'Shea's ship when he arrived, and now only two. Plus, I have the advantage of already knowing the answer. I'm standing beside the answer.

"Shit," Scarlett says. "You sent them all the scans?"

"I had to," I say.

"Yeah, but of their ships as well?"

I shrug. I can almost hear the rock hanging around my neck say: *Dumbass.*

"I'm looking at the scans right now," O'Shea radios to Vlad. *"This don't make no sense."*

"Of course it does, you spawn of a molested sow. You brought her here."

"Fuck," Scarlett says. She fishes into her bag.

"Yeah, let's read a paperback to them," I say. I can already see the two of us in jail together. Unless she wants to say she had a blaster on me the entire time. She would do that for me. No point in both of us going to prison.

Scarlett pulls something out of her bag. "I really don't want to do this, but ending the war is worth more lives than have ever been spilled."

I see what's in her hand. It's a remote detonator. She already has the little clear guard flipped up to expose the silver switch.

"What're you doing?" I ask.

She steps toward the porthole and peers out at the asteroid field. Her body has gone tense. Her shoulders are riding up around her neck. I step toward her, reach out my one good hand.

"I'm sorry," she says.

I hear a faint click. Out in the debris field, an orange cloud blooms like a flower on high-speed film.

"What did you do?"

I think of that animal in its cage. I think of the way it looked at me, water streaming from its jowls. It's strange that I think of the animal before I think of O'Shea. Maybe it's the cage. Maybe I have some affinity for helpless things.

"Vlad was not a good guy," Scarlett says. "He's with the mob. Has done horrible things to decent people."

"Vlad?" I ask. "I thought you came here with O'Shea."

Scarlett crosses the room and stares at one of my screens. "I did. But I only had one bomb. And I kinda like Mitch. I mean, he's a dick, and he's dumb as a sack of sand, but he's not evil."

"What about the kid?" I ask, thinking of the boy who looked at me through his bangs. "What about Vlad's bounty?"

Scarlett turns and looks at me. I can tell she never saw the boy. Probably placed the bomb on the ceiling of Vlad's airlock, right inside the door while we were in the cockpit.

It's what I would've done. She doesn't say anything, doesn't ask me about the kid, just swallows this information as she turns back to the monitors.

"Now where's that other ship?" she asks. "And Mitch is going to be on his way. We'll have to get ready for that."

"*Beacon 23,* Sanity's Edge. *Come in.*"

"Shit," I say. "I've got to get that." I cross over to the HF. Scarlett grabs the mic before I can and squeezes the transmit button to talk to O'Shea. She must've already considered the ruse of commandeering the beacon and saving my ass.

"You've got two minutes to spin up your drive and scoot," she says. "In two minutes, I blow your ship." Narrowing her eyes, she stares out a porthole. "And don't come any closer, asshole."

I turn and follow her gaze; I see the bounty hunter's ship heading our direction.

"*Bullshit,*" O'Shea says. "*You woulda already done it.*"

"I'll kill this beacon operator, then." She lifts an eyebrow at me. Smiles.

"*Fifty million in cold hard cash,*" O'Shea says. "*I'll shoot him for you.*"

"Motherfucker," I say. Scarlett cradles the mic. Is obviously thinking. "That blaster of yours is all we got," I tell her. "There aren't any weapons here. There are two of them out there. And my lifeboat can't go hyper."

"Can we lock them out?" she asks.

"They've got warrants. I know how to override the airlocks to open them in an emergency, but no way to keep them closed, not if they have marshal IDs. I mean, if I had a few hours to really dig into it I could figure something out."

"Then we get the jump on them," she says. "We get down there and wait."

I stare at the radio. O'Shea hasn't said a thing since offering to shoot me dead. I think about that animal on his boat; did he say it was a warthen? He could probably turn that thing loose on us and just smoke a cigar and wait for the screaming to stop. I pull out the bounty sheet and unfold it. Study the fine print. "Fifteen mil just for locating you," I say. "He doesn't even have to come in here. He'll just call it in and wait for the cavalry. You shouldn't have come for me. What were you thinking?"

Scarlett ignores this last bit. Instead she says, "I know Mitch. For an extra thirty-five mil, he's coming in. We should get down there."

She heads toward the ladder. I feel like pointing out that it might take him an extra fifteen minutes to dock. But I see out the porthole that he's hauling ass our way. And we've got fifty-six rungs between us and the lock collars. Before I hurry after Scarlett, I de-energize the two free collars. He should be able to use his credentials for an override, but it'll take a few moments before he figures out he needs to.

Scarlett is down the first ladder and on to the second before I even get started. I barely feel my sprained ankle thanks to the rush of adrenaline, but the arm is still useless. I go down gingerly, remembering the time I slipped off a rung, caught my chin on the ladder, and nearly bit clear through my tongue. In my living quarters, I grab a blanket and a shirt and throw them down the next ladder. More rungs. I can feel O'Shea getting close. I can hear Scarlett below, calling for me to hurry. In the next module, I grab a roll of duct tape from where I was working on my project earlier that day. Was it just that day? Seems like forever ago. Time flies with company. I toss the blanket, shirt, and tape down the last ladder and start my last descent.

"What's this?" Scarlett calls out, as the items rain down.

"Didn't you see that thing on his ship? This is so it doesn't chew us in half." I reach the bottom of the ladder, grab the shirt, and try wrapping it around my forearm with my teeth. Scarlett sees what I'm after and does it for me, holstering the blaster. She uses the duct tape to secure the wrap, tearing the tape with her teeth. It's strange, but I want to kiss her right then. Maybe just in case anything happens.

"I was thinking maybe we could bag it with the blanket," I say. "If I was him, I'd send it through the door first. Try and scare us shitless."

There's a bang against the beacon. Fuck. He's already here. I hear a screech and a scrape as he tries to get a lock. But without the electromagnets engaged, there's no grab. It's taking longer for him to figure that out than I thought.

"You take the blaster," Scarlett says, pushing the pistol into my left hand. "I've got two hands for the blanket. Besides, you're a better shot."

"Not with this hand, I'm not."

But she's already got the blanket and is positioning herself beside airlock Bravo, which is where the scraping seems to be emanating from. I glance over at my walk suit, wishing I had time to put it on. I feel unprotected. Like a raw and open wound. And then I hear the collar buzz as O'Shea figures out he needs the override. I also see that I'm a criminal now. Without even considering the alternative, I'm sitting here, ready to blast away at a bounty hunter on legal marshal business. There's a bounty sheet tucked in my waistband. It's for a girl I had sex with a few times amid the fury of war, someone who just happened to be in my squad for half a tour, who is obviously batshit crazy, and who has probably done a lot of illegal stuff, like hacking into navy databases and tracking me down. And I'm just throwing my life and my career away for her? What the hell am I doing?

I look down and realize I'm holding the blaster. Fifty mil. I could sit in miserable solitude on an island in sector one for the rest of my life. I could contemplate my black thoughts every day in paradise. Just need to slide the barrel to the right, away from the door, and onto a woman I once loved.

But the barrel doesn't waver. Not a fraction of an inch. I don't contemplate this thing so much as marvel over the fact that I'm *not* contemplating it. I marvel that I'm so quick to choose the wrong side. This is my legacy, choosing the wrong side. Scarlett knows. She knew before she got here. It's why she came. She knows I didn't set off that bomb on Yata because I couldn't kill all those unborn Ryph. How did she know? How does she know I never killed the Lord who gutted me? Why is she here if she knows I'm a traitor? A traitor with medals and a big fat lie.

The light over the airlock goes green. Holy hell, we're taking on a bounty hunter. Maybe he's as big an idiot as he seems. Or as bad a shot as he is a pilot. The inner door slides open. I crouch behind the ladder, for a little protection and to rest my forearm on a rung and steady my aim. Scarlett is coiled like a spring by the door. As soon as it opens, I see the animal. I can't shoot. I yell instead for Scarlett to *DO IT!* and the blanket twirls in front of the warthen. There's a mad shriek from the animal as it gets tangled up. Scarlett yells for me to shoot it, then something bounces into the room and there's a blinding flash and a deafening roar.

I lose my footing and stumble back from the blast, covering my eyes, but it's too late. I can't see. I fire a shot toward what I hope is the door, and the blaster kicks in my hand. I hear the sizzle of a bolt striking steel. A miss. The world is a red haze with black splotches. A form appears in front of me. Someone grabbing me. Taking the blaster away. It's over.

"Get down," Scarlett says. She's beside me. It's her with the gun. My vision is clearing, and I hear a blaster go off—a bolt strikes the ladder near my hand, the metal sizzling against my palm. I dive to the side as another round hits nearby. I think Scarlett and Mitch are firing at each other. The animal's muffled shrieks tell me it's still tangled. When my vision clears, I see Scarlett holding her arm, smoke rising from a charred wound, Mitch using the airlock as cover and firing at her, and the animal getting free, shaking off the blanket, and crouching as it prepares to lunge.

"Fifty mil alive or dead," O'Shea yells around the corner. "Your choice which."

He sees me and narrows his eyes. He knows. Knows I'm on the wrong side. I can see the headline: *Hero Betrays Federation; Abets Known Terrorist.* Mitch raises his gun at me as the warthen uncoils with a growl and launches toward Scarlett.

I don't know why I think to do this, what part of my subconscious is yelling at me to jump, but it's some part that knows Mitch O'Shea is not a good pilot and probably spends no time away from gravity, that he has a weak stomach. I've only got one good ankle and one free arm, but it's enough. I leap. The blaster round misses. I hit the kill switch taped to the ceiling. The panels in the floor are shut off. Gravity goes away all at once.

O'Shea lurches and retches as his organs spring up inside him. The warthen glances off Scarlett, and both go rebounding. The animal's shriek turns into a confused whimper. O'Shea is turned around and cartwheeling in the airlock. I worry about him getting to his ship, where the grav panels are still on. Grabbing the ladder as I rebound from my jump, I brace my feet against one of the rungs and coil my legs. I've done this a thousand times down the weightless arm to the GWB, barely needing to course correct against the wall. I don't have a gun, but I'm a bullet. Shoving both legs straight, I take off with terrible speed. O'Shea sees me. Tries to swing his blaster around, but it sends him spinning the other way. A bolt lances past me. I crash into him, knocking his air out. But I send us both toward his open ship and gravity.

Mitch goes through first and is sucked to the deck, lands with a clatter and a clang. All that gear. I land on my shoulder and feel it pop back out. The world turns white for a moment, stars blooming and then receding in flashing streaks. Something rolls across the deck. Something round. O'Shea levels his blaster at me. I roll as far from him and the loose grenade as I can. There's a blast, a flash of heat against my face, and I think for a second that I've been shot. But when I look his way, I see O'Shea is mangled. Killed by his own grenade knocked loose in the fall. His body reminds me of so many of my friends. The lifeless, confused gaze, staring off into the distance. They all look the same. Like there's nothing to see there.

CHAPTER 17

Back through the airlock, I embrace the weightlessness. I can't imagine what Mitch felt when the gravity went off. Even when you're used to it, when you feel it a dozen times a day, every time I go down to the GWB to get a buzz, there's that odd sensation of every nerve in my body going from a downward tug to . . . nothing. Like cresting a hill in a speeding car. Or nosing down in atmo. The vertigo is intense if you're not used to it. For poor Mitch O'Shea, it was his end.

The warthen is twisting and howling in the zero-gee. I see Scarlett bracing in the corner of the room, a few feet off the floor, taking aim with her blaster.

"Wait!" I shout.

The blanket is hovering above the deck. I gather it on my trajectory toward the ladder. There's all kinds of debris floating about. My walk suit. Tools. The roll of tape. I send the blanket floating toward Scarlett, and it moves like a wraith through the air. She gathers it. "We just need to get it through the airlock," I tell her.

She nods. Knows I need this. Knows me well enough. The blaster is holstered. I pull myself up the ladder with my free hand. The pain in my shoulder and ankle are distant, muffled like my hearing from the shock grenade and the explosive blast. The cat is whimpering. Doesn't seem so ferocious now. Scarlett opens the blanket and kicks off toward the animal, manages to take it from the back. I push off and hit the switch on the ceiling, bracing myself for the fall. There's a clang as the tools hit the deck, and then a series of *oomph*s as the three of us follow suit. If my ankle wasn't broken before, it feels like it now.

Scarlett looks to have landed on the animal, which is lying still. Barely moving. She drags it in a bundle of fabric to the airlock, wrestles it through. I limp over and key the door. Before it slides shut, I see the warthen extricate itself and dash off into the ship. The fight is out of her. Or maybe without a master to obey, she has no target. Either way, she's trapped on the ship until I figure out what to do.

I sag against the wall, exhausted. Scarlett tries to catch me. My shoulder screams out. My foot won't take any weight. Her hands are on me, her face so close, her lips so familiar, my mind still stunned and racing. She starts to say something, starts to thank me, to tell me she loves me, that we can end all wars, that we can make life, have children, move to sector one, be heroes together—

When her eyes widen in pain. And I see inside those windows into her soul, and I see that she is a good person, deep down, just as the life leaves her. Just before her body sags against mine, nothing left to animate it.

Stepping through airlock Charlie is the bounty hunter in black. She has a whisper gun in her hand. It's pointed right at me. A woman I loved is in my arms, dead. I'm next. I know this with all the certainty of gravity planetside.

The bounty hunter walks to within a pace of me. I'm half pinned under Scarlett's weight and half pinned by my injuries. I can't move. I can't even resist. I've wanted to be dead for so long that I open my arms to the concept, to the idea of not existing. I want it. I feel my entire being open up to the cosmos, wanting all of it to pour inside me, for the emptiness to fill me up, to burst me back into the atoms I'm made of, to be the tinsel and debris of that cargo, all scattered through space, unknowing and unfeeling.

The bounty hunter pulls the blaster from Scarlett's holster and flings it across the module. She grabs Scarlett by the collar and pulls her off me. The woman in black is fiercely strong. She keeps the whisper gun aimed at my head as she drags Scarlett across the deck and through the airlock.

The door closes.

I never heard her come. I barely hear her leave. A light goes from green to red above the door. Scarlett is gone, and I haven't been arrested, haven't been killed, and I'm angry as hell. Depressed and angry as hell and full of conviction. *Conviction.* The missing ingredient. The energy to do it. To finally do it. And nearby, an animal that wants to kill me. So it's not my weak-ass hands refusing to pull the trigger.

I work my way shakily to my feet. Need to do this before I change my mind. Need to embrace my dark secret, the desire to be ended, the unwhisperable, or they'll lock you away. I key open the airlock to O'Shea's ship. "Come and get me!" I shout. The remains of the warthen's owner are ten paces away. I stumble through the airlock, into the ship, hoping to be eaten. The animal turns the corner, and I brace for a world of searing pain, of claw and tooth, of white-hot mercy, but I just feel it brush against me. I open my eyes, didn't realize I'd closed them, and turn to see a tail whisk around the corner. I stumble back into the module, confused. The warthen has a food pack in its mouth. It goes to my walk suit, which is back to a heap on the floor, turns twice in a circle on it, and lies down, chewing on the pack, protein paste going everywhere.

All of this is sensed at a distance. I'm too focused on my dark secret. My new conviction. I hobble toward the other airlock, where Scarlett disappeared. I key open the outer door, step inside the lock, and shut the door behind me. In the tight confines, I think I can smell her. She just passed through here. Was alive moments ago. Now is dead and gone. Her hope has been wiped from the universe.

I wanted to tell her my dark secret. I was so close. More time together, and I would've confessed. I would've told her how I come here every night before I go to sleep, how I stand in one of these airlocks, how I close the door behind me, and how I think about the vacuum of space on the other side.

Every night, I do this.

Without fail.

There's an emergency override code that'll open this door even if there's no atmo on the other side. It's for going on space walks. We're supposed to do one every week. I never have. I only come in here with my suit off. To breathe my last. To end the nightmare.

Leaning against the wall, I enter the first three digits of the override code.

My finger hovers over the fourth.

I've done this every day I've been here. Every single day. But this time I want it. I can't go on.

Three numbers sit on the little screen, waiting.

I touch the fourth.

I touch it, but I can't press it.

I never can.

I sag to the ground, sobbing and broken, hugging my knees.

Bad things come in threes—but then they stop.

And start all over again.

COMPANY

CHAPTER 18

A billion stars in the night sky—and one of them is winking at me.

Except this flashing light is not a star. A hundred or so klicks away, it belongs to what looks like another beacon, similar to mine. It appeared a month ago when a tug came out of hyperspace and parked it there. I wasn't sure if it was going to stay or move on—sometimes these commercial tugs use my remote bit of space as a way station. But this morning, the beacon went operational. It seems I have a neighbor.

I pinged NASA on the QT, but all they'll say is that the cargo wreck a few months back signaled the need for some *redundancies*. It reminds me of an intersection in my hometown in Tennessee that got by just fine with stop signs until a chicken truck plowed into that young couple. Our first stoplight went up a few weeks later. That stoplight blinked yellow all night, in deference to the quiet, and the adults about town discussed with grave voices what this unwanted intrusion might mean.

A hundred klicks away, a light blinks at me. I know what it means. It's a cold reminder of my failure. Of wreckage spilled and lives lost. If stop signs could feel shame, I imagine that one in my hometown felt something like this. Standing there, frozen, watching in horror as that young couple got killed, feathers and dead chickens everywhere, all that squawking, until weeks later someone in an orange vest pulls that sign out of the ground and strings up the newfangled.

My warthen nuzzles against me, probably because of these guilt-laden thoughts. Her name is Cricket. She's like a cross between a Labrador and a leopard, with moods just as wild as those two extremes. There was a time when she wanted to kill me, but now she just follows me around like a puppy. I'm pretty sure warthens are empaths, that they pick up on moods and even some thoughts. When the bounty hunter who owned her died, she glommed onto me. That's probably not a good thing, with thoughts as dark as mine.

I'd love to know more about these creatures, but there's scant information in the archives, and I can't exactly send off a research request to Houston. Here's how *that* conversation would go:

> Station Operator: "Sir, could you come here for
> a minute? I've got . . . well, let's just say it's an
> unusual re-rec from 23."

Chief of Ops: "Lemme see. Hmm. Wants to know about warthens, eh? Hey, isn't this the guy with the pet rock?"

SO: "Yessir. Same guy. I've also got this completely unrelated issue with his beacon. I mean, I'm sure these two things have absolutely nothing to do with one another, nothing whatsoever, but O2 consumption has gone up fifty percent throughout his beacon, and our boy is going through food packs twice as fast as usual."

CO: "And now he wants a feeding and care guide for a large alien quadruped known to be in the employ of bounty hunters?"

SO: "That's right, sir."

CO: "Didn't this guy have a run-in with some bounty hunters recently?"

SO: "I believe so, sir. He's had quite a shift."

CO: "Any chance the O2 and food pack problem started right around the same time as the bounty hunter thingy?"

SO: "You know, sir, now that you mention it, I do believe both issues started around the same time. Same day, in fact."

CO: "I see."

SO: "..."

CO: "..."

SO: "..."

CO: "Yeah, I got nothing either. Send him whatever he wants."

Okay, that last bit is wishful thinking. And yeah, I have conversations like these in my head a lot. But at least I don't have them out loud anymore. Not as much, anyway.

Cricket rubs her nose against my arm, and I lift it so she can tuck her head against me. I point at the blinking light. "There," I tell her. "Do you see it? What do you make of that?"

The two of us watch as the black of space swallows the light, spits it out, then swallows it again. I stare at the beacon, mesmerized. Cricket paws at her reflection.

So many questions. Is someone over there? Another operator? I've tried the HF twice, with no response. And NASA doesn't like us to use the QT for non-emergencies, so I haven't been pestering Houston every five seconds like I want to. Instead, I've been up here in the GWB, watching this solitary light flash on and off. I've been watching it for hours. How in the world did I pass the time before this intrusion into my routine? When the stars were all fixed, time slid by unnoticed. But now there's a metronome out there, tick-tick-ticking the day ever so slowly away.

The thought of ticking reminds me to check the time. It's 2228 local. There's an army troop transport, bound for the front lines, due to pass through soon. A ship full of guns and the men and women to fire them. Rows and rows of heroes. I remember wearing my fatigues and boarding commercial ships to get back to my company from R&R, how people would thank me and pat me on the back and how good it felt to board a plane before first class. Respect. Only because they had no idea what I did out there. If they did, they would've been clutching their children, not sending them over to thank me.

I also remember catching the eye of the few conscientious objectors in the terminal, the people opposed to the war but afraid to speak up. There was no hate in their eyes, only pity. Sadness. Knowledge that I might be necessary, but that we shouldn't be *proud* that I was necessary. That's how I saw myself and my company by the end of my second tour. I didn't hate what we did so much as hate the need for it all. No one should applaud this. We should bow our heads not in thanks but in sadness.

I give the lighthouse keeper in the photograph a nod, my colleague from a different era. Then I stick my head into the long chute leading to the beacon proper. With a single pull from the edge of the tube, I launch myself down.

Or across.

Or up.

Direction loses meaning for the few seconds it takes to reach gravity on the other side. I twist in the air, pull my feet under me, bend my legs, fall through into the command module, and land in a crouch—precisely the type of hotshot maneuver the labcoats warned me never to try. Which gave me the idea in the first place.

I get out of the way quickly before Cricket lands right where I was standing. She shakes her head and grunts. Still hates the vertigo, but hates being away from me even more. Hates it enough that she's learned how to scramble up and down the ladders, and even figured out how to paw her way through the weightless chute.

I have to admit, having her around is nice. That's probably why I hid her up in the GWB when the navy came to haul off the bounty hunter's ship and the bounty hunter's lifeless corpse. After they left, I found her acting loopy up there, which must mean the GWB messes with her head just like it does mine. For all I know, it's worse for her. She can pick up on thoughts, or pheromones, or *something*. Maybe her brain is just more sensitive. All I know is that NASA still has me on quarantine, and here I am taking in aliens.

Like I said, I'm not very good at this job.

The debris across the asteroid belt attests to that.

Makes me wonder if NASA's putting this new beacon in not for mechanical backup but for *personnel* redundancy. Maybe my being a great big war hero makes it difficult for them to recall me. Maybe they hope this'll be my outpost for life, somewhere out of the way. Maybe this beacon is my pension plan. My forced retirement. Where they put heroes who have nothing left to give.

Cricket growls at me for thinking these things, and I force away the shadowy thoughts. That's the good thing about having a warthen around. It's why I've stopped thinking about jumping out the airlock with no helmet on.

The last time I sat in front of the airlock door and keyed in the first three digits of the override code was the day I adopted this strange creature. The next time I even *thought* about going down there, Cricket acted like she was going to maul me. Paced around the ladder hissing and growling and swiping at me if I approached her. Maybe this is the ideal remedy for depression: a gun that can read your mind and is forever pointed at your head. Gives you some good practice in bottling up those dark wishes.

Of course, bottling shit up doesn't fix what's ailing you at the core. But I've given up on the idea that anything can fix what ails me.

I check the scanners and readouts across the command dash, then glance at the time again. The troop transport is due. I wait, standing at attention. My old company is on this ship, some of the brothers and sisters I bled with, the few who are still alive, still serving, still have all their limbs. As soon as I see the faint ripple across the grav scanner, I salute them. The ones I let down. The ones I betrayed. And all the ones who can't be on that ship anymore.

I told Scarlett the truth of my heroism right before she died. I told her that I could've taken out a hive of alien buggers with the press of a button. I could've killed billions of them. The blast would've taken out me and two companies of troopers as well, but companies have died for far less. I might've turned the tide in sector six. Eight planets have fallen since then, and the war is pushing through sector seven and heading this way right now. The Ryph are on the offensive.

But for one day, we saw them in retreat. The day I won my medal. The day I did nothing. All I did was wimp out when I could've killed all those unborn monsters. It just seemed to me, in that moment, that the hive was full of little buggers who hadn't done anything wrong yet.

Guess I'm not very good at the big picture stuff. I can barely maintain this little tin can that's become my world. I'm nothing more than a washed-up soldier from a small town in a backwoods corner of an old planet who managed to become a beacon operator.

And not a very good one.

19
CHAPTER

Cricket whines and turns in circles, and at first I think it's from me being hard on myself, but I've never seen her act quite like this. I notice as she turns that she keeps glancing at one of the portholes. Maybe she can feel the troop transport passing by, that carrier filled to the brim with dark thoughts. I go to the porthole and peer out, craning my neck to look down the length of the asteroid field.

At first I don't notice it. It's not until the long flashes come that I realize the beacon isn't so much winking anymore as palpitating. Dot-dot-dot. Dash-dash-dash. Dot-dot-dot.

S.O.S.

Cricket mews.

"I see it," I tell her.

I grab the HF and key the mic. "Unknown beacon operator, this is beacon 23, is everything okay over there? Over."

I wait. The QT is still showing the last message from NASA. I key in: *SOS w neighbr*, then hit "Send," "Confirm," and "Yes I'm goddamn sure."

I wait.

I watch the light.

Two or three seconds go by.

I could pace in circles and wait for NASA to tell me to check it out, but you don't need orders when there's a distress call in space. I served in the navy before I was forced groundside. If anyone hails for help, you help them. None of us could survive out here without a system like this in place.

So by the time my operator in Houston is seeing my message and setting down his coffee and wiping his ridiculous mustache, my feet are already hitting the living module deck one level down, my palms burning from the fast slide. The next ladder drops me into the life support module, then one more ladder takes me to the lock collars. I grab my walk suit and helmet from their hangers and dash inside the lifeboat. Before I can key the door closed, Cricket bounds down from the module above, landing on the grating like a large cat.

"Stay," I tell her, holding out my palm. "Stay."

Cricket tilts her head and cries. She takes a step toward the lifeboat.

"No," I say. "You stay."

Normally she does whatever I ask, or whatever I really concentrate on her doing. But this is one need she seems to always put before mine: the need to follow me. Before I can give her another order, or lock her out, she dashes through the open airlock door, brushing against my leg, nearly knocking me over. By the time I get the airlock secured and get up to the cockpit, she's sitting in the navigator's seat, peering through the canopy like she knows we're going somewhere, like she's done this a thousand times. Or maybe like she knows what happens next.

•••

I wiggle into my walk suit while the autopilot steers us toward the beacon. The throttle is at max, which ain't much in this bucket. And maybe now's a good time to admit that I haven't been in a very good state lately. But this is progress, I think, to realize I'm going a bit mad. The dangerous phase is when that's happening and you can't see it. When you *think* you're sane, so the crazy is all invisible. The reason I wear a rock around my neck is to be reminded of my propensity to lose my grip on reality. Rocky hasn't uttered a peep in a while. I'm getting better, I swear.

I glance over at Cricket, and another thought occurs. What if I'm overstating the whole mind-reading thing? What if I'm making up a pattern of when she nuzzles me and when she doesn't? And here's the truly fun part about going a little crazy: even the obviously sane things you do can be called into question. Is that beacon in front of me real? Did Scarlett really come back into my life, tell me I could help her win the war, and then disappear again? There's a faint stain on the deck by lock collar Charlie, and I can't tell if it's rust or her blood.

I reach over and pet the warthen. There's no doubting this, at least. This is real. And the beacon ahead of me looks pretty damn real. I leave the thrust at full to close the distance, and my mind drifts back to my army days. I can feel the wake of the troop ship that passed through, all those boys and girls heading for the front to be dumped into a trench. I feel the recoil of my rifle as it takes a life. Geysers of soil explode into the air and fill our nostrils. There's the metallic odor of blood as soldiers with hope cry for a medic, soldiers without hope cry for their mommas, and soldiers with guns bring tears to the other side.

I wonder what Scarlett meant by us ending this war. Wars like this don't end until one side is ground to dust. It's crazy to me that naïve people like Scarlett even exist, that they can live in this galaxy, see what we all see, and cling to foolish notions like they do. And yet there are legions of them. Protestors. Picketers. Alien-lovers. Conscientious objectors. Traitors.

Yeah, I'm a traitor. But I'm the worst kind. I don't believe like the rest of them do. I just got tired of it all. I couldn't fight anymore. You fight because your squad needs you to. When the last man standing beside you goes down, you don't need a bullet to take out your knees; the depression does that for you. I've seen the biggest troopers felled by the heavy darkness. I've watched them curl up in the mud and just stop moving. I remember hoping that'd never be me. And here I am.

There's a number on the side of the beacon. I can read the large blocky digits as I close to within a couple klicks: 1529.

Damn.

When I see that number, I don't think of how many beacons there are out there. I don't do the dollar math and think of the poor taxpayers. I don't get all cosmic and think of how big this galaxy is and how much we're spreading out into it. No, I think of how many people are out there, living alone like me.

Too many.

Approaching within a klick of the beacon, which is still flashing its SOS, I can't see anything obviously wrong with it. There's no atmosphere jetting from an impact hit. No orange glow across any of the portholes from a fire inside. In fact, the beacon is obscenely pristine. There's not a char mark on her. Just unblemished, beautiful steel painted NASA white with neat rows of rivets and gleaming solar panels that probably run at 100% efficiency compared to my beacon's 48%.

But my beacon isn't the one with the distress signal. Closing to within a hundred meters, I grab the stick and turn the lifeboat sideways while still carrying all that forward momentum. It's a crazy maneuver in a bucket like this. No idea if the side thrusters can even halt my current velocity. I put them on full and eyeball the distance to the lock collar, guiding the approach until I bang into the beacon and hook the magnet with a three out of ten on the pilot-o-meter.

Cricket growls at me like she thinks I'm being generous.

Throwing off my restraints, I leave my seat and hurry to the airlock. As I key open the lifeboat's inner airlock door,

I see the red light flashing above the control panel. There's no atmosphere handshake from the other side. Something is very wrong with this beacon. Closing my helmet, I shut the lifeboat's airlock behind me, keeping Cricket at bay, and then key in the universal override code. I've got a bad feeling as the door to this beacon opens. And even through my helmet and the thick airlock doors, I can hear Cricket howling with fury on the other side—pissed that I'm leaving her, perhaps. Or just knowing that I'm a fool to go.

CHAPTER 20

The lock module is empty. Bare. The hatch to the other lifeboat is open, so I check inside. If there was a loss of atmo, this is where any survivors would go. But this beacon has a lifeless feel. Sterile. Like a vacuum. Any hope of finding someone over here vanishes. The neighbor's Maserati just has its hazards going off. I glance at my O2 levels in the suit and head for the ladder, knowing NASA would at least want me to turn off the emergency signal and investigate. One flight up is the life support and mechanical module. My boots clang on the rungs, the sound muffled by my helmet.

The mechanical module might as well have shrink-wrap on it. Everything gleams. There are no loose wires dangling from all the add-ons and repairs cobbled together over the years. No oil streaks running down the pumps from worn-out seals. No blistered and peeling paint. No rust or signs of age. She's like a shaved-head recruit standing there, holding her neatly folded fatigues, not a scar on her smooth flesh. Gazing at the room around me, all I can think of is the grief to come. All I can see are the bolts whizzing like bullets in the cosmos around us. All I want to do is throw myself over her grav generator and shield it with my body, keeping everything safe, not letting a damn thing touch her—

There's a bang somewhere above me. Distant. Muffled. Like the debris heard me and reached out and slapped this nubile recruit. Like our drill sergeant caught me smiling at her. I grab the ladder leading up to the living quarters and clomp up the rungs. More newness here. I touch the sleep sack. Wish I could pop my helmet open and see what they smell like out of the factory, before dozens of people have slept in them.

Another bang, nearer now. This one startles me, because even through the suit, I can feel that the bang is *inside* the beacon, not against the hull. That's when I notice the duffel bag in the galley. Personal effects. Through the porthole, I can see the *dash, dash, dash* of an open-mouth O as the light outside continues to flash in alarm.

I grab the next ladder and climb up into the command module. I'm not alone. Two legs jut out from under the command dash, sheathed in white NASA sweatpants. Two bare feet. Ten toes splayed upward. Unmoving. Like a body pulled halfway out of a morgue drawer. The upper half of the person is concealed. I think of what it would be like to die like this, asphyxiating, choking on empty, burning lungs. I've thought about that a lot.

I approach the body. *This one's not your fault,* I tell myself. I couldn't have gotten here any quicker. I need to pull the body out to inspect it and determine the cause of death. Reaching down, I grab one of the ankles, and the body spasms. Kicks. There's a shout and a bang. More kicking at me, legs scrambling like they're riding a bicycle, and then hands gripping the edge of the dash, a face appearing, loose strands of hair over wide eyes and an angry mouth. The muffled sound of someone shouting at me: "What the fuck?!"

•••

We stare at one another. It's a woman. Her lips are moving. She has no helmet on, which makes mine feel silly. I reach to open the visor, and there's only a slight twinge of fear that maybe she's an apparition, and maybe I'm not in a beacon at all but out in the cold vacuum of space, and I kinda hope that this is true—

But I breathe atmo when I pop the visor. And I hear the end of her last sentence:

"—the hell'd *you* come from?"

She waits for an answer. This is an easy one. I got this one.

"Beacon 23," I say.

We stare some more. This is awkward.

"I'm— I saw the distress. Are you— Is everything okay?"

"I was just fine until you scared the ever-living shit out of me." The woman brushes some of the loose hair off her face. She's the most beautiful thing I've ever seen. Some distant part of me knows that this is because I've been alone for a long time, and because the last person I loved recently died in my arms, and because I'm just glad this person isn't dead, but there's another part of me that thinks she really might be that gorgeous.

"What's going on?" I ask.

"What's going on? I'll tell you what's going on, those idiots in Texas've built near on two thousand of these buckets, and they still can't send them out without all these glitches. Can't one of these things boot up and work the first time? Is that too much to ask? It must be too much to ask. Hand me that spanner."

There's an open toolkit on the deck, just under the dash. I hand her the spanner, and she ducks back out of sight. My walk suit feels bulky. I shrug under the weight of it all. I feel like taking off my helmet.

"So they sent you out here to operate this thing, and it doesn't even work?" I ask.

"They never work," she tells me. "Not at first." Her voice is a bit muffled by the cavity she's working in, and a bit by my helmet. "And I'm not an operator." She peers out at me from the gloom. "Do I look like an operator to you?"

She looks like a normal person to me. Does that mean "no"? Does that mean I don't look normal? I guess I don't. I decide to leave my helmet on. I've got a week's worth of growth on my chin, and my hair is a shaggy mop that wouldn't pass muster in the army or at NASA.

"I guess not," I say.

"I'm a tuner," she says. "I get these things working so your lot can survive in them. But right now, I'm trying to get all the sensors that're telling this bucket everything's wrong to understand that everything's not wrong. She's all haywire."

"A tuner," I say. It's the first I've heard of them. Sounds like something a piano needs, not a trillion-dollar piece of astral navigation machinery.

The woman leans out of the cavity again, sitting up. Her hair is matted down in places with perspiration. Most of it is in a ponytail. Light brown, with a hint of red. And emerald eyes. I'm an unblinking fool. And the walk suit is damn hot.

"Yes, a tuner," she repeats. "Pass me that bolt, please?"

I break my stare and look where she's pointing. There are small bolts that I recognize, the ones that hold the control consoles to the main panel. I hand her the bolt, but only after slipping one of the lock washers on it. She narrows her eyes at me like she just watched a monkey perform a trick. "I'm Claire." She holds out her hand, which is streaked with grease. I shake it. "What d'you go by?"

I laugh. Nerves, I guess. "Lately, I go by *That Idiot*. In the army, they just called me Soldier. But back in flight school, we were given call signs."

She laughs. "What was your call sign?"

"It wasn't a very good one," I warn.

"Lay it on me. Another bolt, please."

I prep and hand her another bolt. "My call sign was Digger."

Claire's laugh echoes from within the cavity. I shift in place while she works.

"It was supposed to be Tomb Digger," I explain. "Which is . . . you know . . . really badass. But my flight instructor didn't like me, and he saw me rub my nose one time, and said I was a nose digger, and that from then on I'd just go by Digger. So that was it." I shrug, even though she's not looking.

"Tell the truth," she calls out. "You were picking your nose, right? Not just scratching it. Give me the lock nuts."

Her hand emerges. I place the three lock nuts in her palm. "I may have been picking it," I say. "I'm not proud."

"No, you're not. I can tell that about you."

I can't determine if this is a compliment or not. It definitely doesn't *feel* like a compliment.

"So where'd you serve, soldier?"

"All over. Orion. Humbolt. Dakka. Did my first tour on Gturn."

Claire whistles. "They always had you in the shit, didn't they?"

"Hip deep."

She wiggles free from the space, and I move back to give her room. She has on a white NASA tank top. No bra. A trim and muscular physique. Not what I expect in an egghead. She starts working on one of the main consoles, and I watch, following what she's doing. Looks like a master reboot sequence, but she's rewriting the config.sys before it goes through, coding faster than I can type.

"Let's see if this works," she mutters.

The lights go off around us. Pitch black. There's a distant *thunk* from the massive power relays two floors below. Pinpricks of light make themselves known through several of the portholes as my eyes gradually adjust. There's something sensual about this, exhaling and inhaling in that dark space with someone else. I can feel her presence like I have radar. I can tell there's another person in the darkness with me, that I'm not alone. I stand frozen, afraid to move my limbs, afraid of what I might do with them.

The lights come back on. Claire is staring intently at one of the portholes. I look as well. The pulsing, fluttering, palpitating, unsure lights of the shocked and alarmed have returned to that steady metronome, that constant and confident pulse.

Claire smiles at me.

"Much better," she says.

I agree.

CHAPTER

(21)

Cricket pounces on me as I enter the lifeboat. She holds me against the deck, massive paws on my chest, and growls and growls. Clamping down on my arm with her mouth, she squeezes like she wants to bite me. But she just holds me there, making threatening noises in her throat.

I let her have it out and scratch her neck. Relenting, she lets go, mews at me, then licks my face through my open visor.

"I know, I know," I tell her, stroking her head, trying to calm her down. "I'm sorry. Everything's okay. I'm sorry."

I exude these thoughts. Cricket lowers her weight against me, as if we're going to lie just outside the airlock and take a nap.

"Up," I say. "We gotta go. Can't abandon our station. Everything's okay here."

Better than okay. But I can't stay. After an hour of watching Claire work, sweating in my walk suit, feeling useless and awkward, I had to beg my leave. Despite every craving in every cell of my body, I had to beg my leave.

Cricket and I head back to our beacon at half-thrust. I leave one of the displays set to the rear camera, and I watch the unblemished and new recede as I crawl across empty space toward my rundown home. Cricket is passed out on the seat beside me, her body sprawled over the armrest so that her head can reach my arm, pinning it to my seat with the weight of her exhaustion. Must've worn herself out pacing and fretting while I was gone. When I need to adjust the throttle, I lean across and use my left hand so I don't disturb her. What the hell am I doing? Aiding and abetting a fugitive, and now harboring an alien. This is what happens when they give you medals for breaking the rules: you forget the rules apply to you.

Opening the airlock to my home, I smell the tiredness of the place. The clean atmo in the other beacon cleared my nostrils, and now I can smell that the air I live in isn't foul so much as stale. The scrubbers are doing their job more admirably than I thought. Hell, they're doing their job more admirably than *I* am.

Shedding the walk suit, I head toward the ladder. Cricket seems to read my mind and leaps for it first. She wraps her paws around a rung halfway up, lunges again, and grabs the lip. Elbows jut down as she scrambles, rear legs wheeling, tail corkscrewing. Every time she goes up a ladder, it looks like she might not make it, but she always does. I'm already climbing up behind her, the air cool on my sweaty skin, just my sleep shorts on. Cricket takes advantage of my hands being occupied at the top of the ladder and gets in a lick on my head and one on my cheek before I can ward her away.

"No lick," I tell her, wiping my cheek. I've tried to train this out of her. "Never lick me again," I say, shaking a finger at her. She sits and cocks her head to the side. "Last time. Never again. No licking. I mean it."

Her tail swishes the steel grating. I pat her head. I swear she can read my mind, and yet somehow she doesn't seem to hear a word I say. I scratch behind her ears and ask, "These are just for decoration, aren't they?"

She licks my hand. I don't know why I even try.

Up another ladder, I start the shower pod. I let it steam up inside, the water recycling over and over. When it looks like one of those cig smoking rooms in a spaceport, I crack the door and step through the fog and into the scalding hot. The death and tiredness boils off my skin. I scrub the old cells away, getting at the new me beneath. Soap and lather. I fumble for my razor and run it under the showerhead before rolling it across my face. Little patches of hair elude me. I wash my hair, then turn my back to the jet and just let the heat pound into my spine. Water so damn hot. I pee while standing there, remembering Hank from B Company who used to get angry when anyone did this. One whiff of pee in the showers, and Hank'd go ballistic, looking everywhere for the yellow stream. We'd accuse him of using this as an excuse to go around studying our dicks.

Hank was my best friend in the company—for all of the two weeks he was alive with us in the trenches. It was a long two weeks. There aren't any rules about how long you gotta know someone to know you love them. The army taught me that. You can hate the moment you line up your barrel, and you can love the second you lower it. Back and forth like that. Oscillating grav panels. There's no up or down to the cosmos, just a whole bunch of fucking sideways. Just people loving and hating. And no rules on how long it takes.

I turn off the shower as the heat starts to die down from boiling to mere scalding. My flesh is red. Steam rises off me as I leave the pod. Cricket is fast asleep on my bed; she wakes long enough to glance at me, to make sure she isn't missing anything, then goes back to sleep.

I rifle through my clothes, sniffing everything. All the same degree of mildly clean. It's only now that I see the amber light flashing over my bunk. Damn. Message on the QT. I go up the ladder two rungs at a time and check the display. Three messages from NASA asking me to report back in about the SOS.

I key in the number 55. Then I press through three screens of warnings before the entangled particles tickle their entangled twins back in Houston. Five by five is what someone used to say back in some other time to mean that everything is okay. Not sure why this is any more efficient than just saying OK. It probably has something to do with the state of Oklahoma. All their fault. Just like it's Germany's fault we have to say the number nine as "niner." Everyone causes trouble. It's not just me.

I turn the message alarm off and walk a big circle around the command module. Then another circle. Cricket wakes up below, realizes I'm gone, and arrives at the command module with two leaps, a grunt, and some kicking. She curls up on the blanket I leave under the dash for her and watches me pace.

I shake my arms like they're still wet, like there's something in them I need to get out, like those nerves a soldier feels before a big push out of the trenches. What the hell is wrong with me? A trickle of water runs down my breastbone, leaking from the porous rock I wear around my neck. I wipe this away, cross to the porthole, and watch the flashing light for a while. I turn to the HF, wondering what I would say if I picked it up. I turn back to the light.

This is worse than being completely alone.

CHAPTER

22

I dream of my company that night. My old company. B
Company.

Bravo, boys.

Take a bow.

Clap Company.

The kind of clap you don't want to receive.

They cured that shit centuries ago, but they still called us
the VD crew. Very Desperate. Veterans Disabled. Vaginas
& Dicks. Vapor Dust. But my favorite: Verily Dead.

You need one company set aside for the glory runs and
photo-ops. That's not us. That would be the Alpha Company
boys and girls. They think they're the shit, because they get
the milk runs. Might *seem* like they get the worst targets,
the toughest assignments, but they're the targets with all
the intel, the battles we know we can win. A good chess
player doesn't send out the queen unless he knows she's
gonna take a couple pawns and not take a nick. So the top

scorers, the squeaky clean, the square-cut jaws, the Aces and Champs, they get sent out with the best gear and the best air support and the best artillery crews and the biggest budgets, and they always get their buggers.

Charlie Company is for those you barely trust with a gun. The swinging barrels in a crowded dropship that have you ducking so fast you throw your back out.

That leaves Bravo Company, the expendables who know what they're doing. When you've gotta hit something, and you don't know its soft spot, you clap twice for Company B.

SIR YES SIR! SIR, MOTHERFUCKING RIGHT, SIR! SIR, AIM ME AND FIRE, SIR!

We think on our boots in Company B. We fight our way, bewildered, through the confusion and the haze. We don't make it out the other side, not all of us. But somewhere, there's the click of a pen, a proud signature, a father's hand on a young man's shoulder, and we reload. That's the sound of our collective gun cocking, the click of that pen. That's us racking another round in the chamber. Fire that boy out, hope you hit something. If he gets three before he goes home in his own bag, then the numbers look good. That father gets his medal. No one else to wear it. Goes in a frame above the mantel, and on holidays glasses are raised. First you raise the kids, and then you raise a toast.

I see it all in my dreams; I see it every night. The shrapnel seems to come from the earth. When the kinetic missiles hit, the ground vomits hot death. An eruption of soil, a cloud of screaming metal reaching out for the unfortunate, grabbing limbs and lives with abandon.

I see the boys and girls in my dreams. The brothers and sisters. I see the mangled. I see my best friend Hank, who hated when I peed in the shower, and he's standing there with his trousers wet, looking at me, dumbfounded, like he'd shrug at it all if he had the limbs, like the cosmos would be a funny place if that was pee all over him.

"—just need a quick hand."

Yes, we all need a hand. Titanium. Carbon fiber. Neurologically integrated. Five hundred and twelve degrees of hot and cold sensitivity. Better than the real thing. Everyone needs a hand. And a leg. And a new colon. I have half mine. I have a goddamn semicolon. I'm naked in class, and Mrs. Phister is asking me a question about grammar. I pee myself while the kids laugh. There are shower nozzles everywhere, shooting soil and shrapnel into the classroom. Kids laughing and dying. I remember the rule for semicolons; the sentences on both sides have to be full ones. Full people. Whole. Not many of them anymore.

"You listening?"

I'm listening. I'm paying attention. I have no idea what's going on, but I'm paying attention. I take it all in slack-jawed, assuming the guy next to me knows what he's doing. I'll follow him. Someone else is following me.

"Digger? Hello? Soldier, you there?"

I wake up in my sleep sack. There's a squawk of noise from the module above me. Cricket has her head across my chest, is snoring softly. As I blink away the nightmare, she stirs and peers at me from half-lidded eyes. "Shit," I say. "Up. Gotta get up."

I crawl out of the bag, even as Cricket tries to stop me, her head weighing a ton, a paw on my arm. I run naked to the ladder and scramble up, banging my knee and cursing. Snatching the mic, a little breathlessly and a lot desperately, I wheeze, "Yeah— Hello? Hey. I'm here. Wassup?"

I gulp and exhale and suck in a deep breath. Then I remember to add: "Over."

"You okay?" Claire radios back.

"Me? Yeah." Gulps of air. "I'm great. Whatcha need?"

"Shit. I woke you up, didn't I? What's the time here? I'm still on Houston time. Hell, I'm always on Houston time. You wanna check in with me in the morning? Your morning? Over."

I could listen to her babble like this forever. I get ships passing through now and then, get to chat with traders and ore tug captains. They give me sports scores and war updates, which often sound like much the same thing. But this is someone right next door who is staying there, who goes to sleep and wakes up there. A mere hundred klicks away.

"No, I'm up," I promise her. "How can I help?"

I'll wear my good clothes this time. I rub my face, feeling the smooth skin. Sniff my armpit.

"I need you to give me a full sweep with your gwib. Trying to calibrate this bucket, but there's so much debris here. Can't clear the noise."

Yes, the debris. That would be my fault. I did that. Sorry.

"Yeah, sure," I say, disappointed that it's something I can do from here. "No problem." I go to my dash and power up the GWB for a full pulse. The lights dim a little while the massive capacitors two modules down charge up. I try to picture Claire standing over there, looking at her own console, watching and waiting. I see her in her sweatpants and tank top. Her hair in a ponytail. A few loose strands tucked behind her ear. Reddish hair. The color of rust.

"Whenever you're ready," she says.

When the PULSE OK light goes green, I flip the metal toggle beneath it. There's a sensation of vertigo, like the grav panels beneath my feet are on the fritz, but it's just a wave of whatever makes me feel nice and numb when I rest my head against the GWB. A megadose. The light goes red for a moment and then shuts off altogether. Cricket grunts at me.

"Looks good," Claire radios. *"Muchas gracias. If there was a bar within spittin' distance, I'd buy you a drink."*

I stare at the mic in my hand. I glance over at Cricket, then toward the chute and the business end of my beacon. Knowing I shouldn't, but that I'm going to anyway, I squeeze the mic.

"I've got something even better," I say.

CHAPTER 23

Claire is waiting for me at the lock collar. The split second the outer door of my lifeboat opens, I realize that she's gonna see me for the first time, without the helmet, with my hair way out of regs, and with my gaunt face.

Whatever she's thinking, she manages a smile. The cramp in my cheeks is a hint for me to not smile back quite so much.

"Beacon warming present," I say, holding out a black plastic bag.

Claire looks at it quizzically, but accepts. There's a length of red wire twisted around the top of the bag. It's the kind of bag our air filters come in. I'm supposed to toss them in the recycler, but Cricket loves batting them around the modules.

"If this is wine, I'm gonna want to know where you got it from," she says.

I watch as she twists the wire off and opens the bag. Reaching inside, she pulls out the can of WD-80.

"You can never have enough," I explain. "And I noticed the circ fan was squeaking a little the last time I was here."

She laughs. "You're sweet." The words hit me like a knee to the gut.

"Yeah, well." I point awkwardly at the can. "It's a good year, too."

"And this is supposed to be better than a beer?" she asks.

"Oh, no, I just wanted to bring you something. The . . . uh, follow me?"

I step past her, and she closes the airlock behind me. I take the ladder first. The pristine nature of the beacon hits me just as hard this time. The two beacons are like their occupants, I guess. One flawless. The other horribly disfigured.

Up in the command module, I duck my head inside the long tunnel that leads off to the GWB. With a swimming motion from my arms, and a good leap, I launch myself down the chute, spiraling a little so the handholds are above and below me, smooth walls to either side, my fingertips brushing the surface to keep me centered. At the other end, I hit the gravity generated by the floor of the GWB module. I turn and wait for Claire. She's right behind me, gliding through space, upside down, so that her worried frown matches my smile.

She catches herself at the edge of the chute and aligns herself to gravity, then lowers herself like a gunner gets in her tank. The space is tight for two. With Cricket, it's never a worry, as she tries to curl up in my lap. With Cricket, it's comfortable. Here, it's overtly intimate. I wonder if this is why I brought her here. Then I remember why I brought her here. I move over and sit with my back to the GWB, patting the grating beside me. "Sit," I say. And by habit, it sounds too much like I'm talking to Cricket. "If, you know . . . you want to."

She settles in beside me.

"I don't know why it does this, but just rest your head back against the dome and relax. You should feel it. Like a sip of whiskey."

We both sit there for a few breaths. Inhale. Exhale. Inhale. The unblinking stars peer in through the porthole.

"Do you feel it?" I ask.

Claire doesn't answer at first.

"Yeah," she whispers. "I . . . I think so."

We sit like that for what feels like a few minutes. That's an eternity to sit with a stranger in silence. I feel a nice numbness creep into my bones. I feel my mind relaxing, words coming to me, tumbling out between my lips like soldiers from a trench.

"Whadja do before you became a tuner?" I ask. I'm assuming she was an engineer. In maintenance or assembly. One of those egghead roles.

"Same as you," she says, her voice a little quiet and distant. "Army. Two tours."

This tries to register, but doesn't quite. She's too clean for that. Too pure.

"I enlisted after Delphi," she adds.

"Yeah," I say. "I guess a lot of people did. You see any action?"

Claire doesn't answer.

I hate myself as soon as the words leave my lips. Like a general regretting his orders, watching his men run out of the trenches in the wrong direction. If she hasn't seen action, it sounds like I'm judging her. If she has, I'm stirring up memories best left settled in the bottom of her soul.

"I was on Yata for the push," she tells me, her voice quiet. "A Company. Second platoon."

No way, I think to myself. *No fucking way*.

"We were pinned down for three weeks. They were bombing us to oblivion. Then this squad with a death wish pushes into the hive, threatens to blow it all to smithereens, and—" She glances over at me, gives me a long, cold look. "I'm sure you know the rest."

Of course I do. Everyone does. But all I can think is: *Not her*. Even though I know this is no great coincidence. All of A and B companies were there for the push. For the five weeks I was Earthside, after I got out of the VA, I had people coming up and shaking my hand, thanking me, saying I saved them. And when the tears came to their eyes, I'd nod and tell them it wasn't necessary. Just doing my job. Lie through my teeth. Tell them the same damn story. Over and over until you almost believe it.

"I wouldn't take you for a soldier," I whisper, my voice cracking a little. "You seem too . . . good for that."

"Yeah," Claire says. "Aren't we all."

•••

"You didn't bring libations, but thanks for the lubrication," she tells me, smiling, as I board the lifeboat. "I'm sure the grease'll come in handy as I get this bucket up and running."

"No problem," I say.

It feels like the close of a date. Like she's walking me to my car. A whiff of distant and forgotten normalcy drifts by. It's like that pocket of warm water that comes out of nowhere when you're swimming in a lake, or that ray of sunshine on a cloudy day, or that smile from that woman behind the counter at the DMV. The unexpected and bright. The startling joy.

"Hey—" she says, as I turn to go.

I turn back. Is she going to kiss me? We're both soldiers, and sex was something that soldiers engaged in as casually as they tore into MREs. Just a thing. I don't want it to ever be a thing like that again.

"Do you need anything?" she asks. Her brow is knitted together. Lines of worry across her face.

"Like what?"

"Well, I've got a few days here—" She jabs her thumb back at her beacon. "—then I'm back to Houston for a bit for a debrief. If there's anything you need over on 23 . . ."

I laugh. "My can needs more than Houston's got," I say. "Besides, their engineers were up here a few months ago. Just made the place worse. Had the grav panels oscillate on me—"

"Shit. Really?"

"Oh, yeah. So don't let them send any help my way. I'm good."

"Okay."

There's something else. Something she wants to ask. Something she's too kind to say.

"Okay," she says again.

And I know that look. That worry. I know what she's wondering. What she wants to say.

If you ever need anyone to talk to . . .

Like talking ever fixed anything. Like words have that power. I touch the rock around my neck, knowing I've got plenty who'll listen, but none who understand.

"I'll see ya," I say, turning my back before I make a mess of things.

"Yeah," Claire says, like she knows better.

It's only after the door hisses shut that I pick up on what she said. Back to Houston in a few days. That's all. Just that pocket of warmth in a freezing lake. Just a glancing ray of sunshine. A star that winks once, twice, then turns away. Death without the dying.

CHAPTER

24

By the end of my first tour of duty, I was already an asshole. I told myself I'd never get like that. I remember when I joined my first company, after losing my wings and being put in the trenches, how I'd introduce myself to someone with too many days of service, and they wouldn't take my hand, wouldn't give me a name, would simply tell me to "Fuck off."

I called them the assholes. It's what I muttered to myself as they walked away. I later learned that this exchange wasn't what it seemed. You shake enough hands and meet enough people and lose them all to the war, and you get to where you don't want to meet anyone else. Looking back, I can see how the assholes were quick to give me any advice that might keep me alive, but they didn't say shit about who they were. Names were simply home states or cities or favorite ball teams or embarrassing nicks. The assholes didn't hate you; they just didn't want to get attached. I got like that. I didn't want to ever meet another Hank. I think that's why he remained my best friend throughout my two and a half tours. I never let anyone else get so close. Those two weeks were painful enough. Hell, after Scarlett, I never confused sex and love again. Used to think the two had something to do with one another. But then the sex and dying came so close together that it almost felt like you were doing it with a corpse. Takes the joy out of it. You die a little inside every time you have joyless sex. Neurons prune back. The good in there withers. And some things never grow back.

This is why I spend the next two days staring at the HF, too self-protecting to pick it up, too enamored to just walk away. I don't want to know another thing about her. I can already feel the agony of her leaving, off to another brand-new beacon, asking someone to pass her a bolt, the smell of soap and grease on her skin, bonding with some other soldier, leaving behind a dotted line of finely tuned machines and shattered hearts. Makes me feel sorry not just for myself, but for every other lonely and hapless vet who—

"Hello . . . ?"

Cricket lifts her head from her blanket and stares at the ladder well. What the hell? What the hell?

Looking over at the airlock indicators, I can see that collar Bravo is energized. Who the hell stops over unannounced like this? I step toward the ladder, step back, step toward it again, my arms out and akimbo, while Cricket gets up from her blanket.

Before I can think to stop her, the warthen bounds for the ladder.

"Fuck," I say. I run after her. "Stop! Wait! No!" All the useless commands come out together in a jumble. I practically jump down the ladder, landing in a roll and grabbing at Cricket, but she's already leaping down another level. I don't stop to put on pants or a shirt, just have my boxers on, and I'm down the next ladder to the life support module when I hear a scream just below me. A shriek. I land to find Claire on her back, Cricket standing with her paws on the tuner's chest, holding her against the grating.

"Off!" I shout, pushing Cricket to the side and ending up on my knees. Cricket tries to get at Claire again—I can't tell if it's to greet her or dominate her—and I fight to hold the alien back. Claire scoots until she's against the air scrubber and pulls her knees up against her chest, is staring at the animal wide-eyed, her jaw hanging open.

"Sorry," I say, sitting down and reaching out toward Claire. "I'm so sorry."

She doesn't say anything. I tell Cricket to back off, to go lie down, to take it easy, and finally the tension goes out of her muscles. She paces back and forth on the other side of me, her head tracking Claire. I keep pointing to the grate, telling her to lie down, *thinking* for her to lie down, and she finally does. But with a grunt. Like she'd rather be doing anything else.

"God, I'm so sorry," I say. I reach over and touch Claire's shin, remembering the time I touched her ankle. She startles, but not as bad as the last time.

"What the hell *is* that?" she asks.

"A warthen," I say, breathing hard from the dash down. I rub the ankle I sprained a while back. "I— She sorta adopted me."

"That's—" Claire can't take her eyes off Cricket. She aims a finger at the animal. "That's against regs. That's . . . You can't have that."

"I know," I say. "I know. I suck at this job. You're gonna can me. I know. We can go QT Houston if you like."

I almost feel relief at this. Lately, I've gone from thinking I'll serve in this bucket for the rest of my life to being pretty sure I could be fired at any moment. This is the route I took when I sided with Scarlett against the bounty hunters. But the only person who knows that is the hunter who dragged Scarlett's body away. And she hasn't said a thing, apparently. But with Cricket around, it's just a matter of time. When they do the food resupply, they'll figure it out. NASA counts every hundred-dollar bolt. They won't miss this. And now they know. The jig is up.

"What the hell is it?" Claire asks. While I'm considering which remote planet I'll retire on, she seems to be coming out of shock. "Canine? Feline?"

"Neither," I say. And I see that the fear is out of her, replaced by curiosity. Here's a soldier who's seen a shelling. Knows when to duck for cover and when to come out, look around, see who needs help.

I snap for Cricket, who bounds up like a coiled spring, has only been lying there because I yelled at her to. She nearly knocks me over on her way to Claire, gets both paws around her neck, and starts licking her hair.

"Down!" I say.

"Easy," Claire tells the animal.

And I see that Claire can hold her own. She twists to the side and rolls the warthen on her back. Pins her there, which I know from experience isn't easy. Cricket's body is tense, but her legs settle as Claire finds that spot on her belly.

"She likes that," I say.

"Who wouldn't?" Claire asks.

We stare at each other.

This is the last goddamn thing I wanted. The last goddamn thing.

"What the hell are you doing here?" I ask, unable to censor myself, angry at her for being a good person and shoving it in my face like this, waving it around like a flag, making me notice.

"Fuck you," she says, but she keeps rubbing Cricket's stomach. It's just trench talk. Soldier anger, which lasts as long as soldier love does. "You said this bucket was falling apart, I thought I'd come see if I could help. But I think maybe the bucket isn't what's broken."

"The hell does that mean?" I ask.

She looks down at Cricket, whose eyes are closed. She's doing that deep growling thing that I'd call a purr if it wasn't so goddamn unsettling.

"You're right," she says. She pats Cricket, then unfolds her legs and stands to go. "Good luck with everything, soldier."

"Wait," I say. I reach for her hand, even though I don't know her, even though I've spent all of four hours with her, even though I haven't thought of anything else for the last three days. "I'm sorry." Two words that I used to choke on when I was younger, that I only now know the value of, the true worth, and how good they feel to say. "It's just—"

"What?" she asks. She's standing there, my hand around her wrist, looking down at me. Cricket is watching us both.

"It's just that—"

I shake my head.

"You don't want to have feelings for me because you're scared I'm gonna leave?" she asks.

I turn away, because the tears leap up in me so fast that my throat closes and I can't swallow or see. I wipe at my eyes, full of shame.

"Well fuck you, soldier. We all leave. Every one of us. You've been in the shit. You choose to keep yourself from people who might leave, you choose to keep yourself alone. We all go. Fucking open up to someone. For your own sake."

Cricket's head is in my lap. She's looking up at me. Claire is peering down at me. I'm the rock between two soft spots.

"You think I don't hurt?" Claire asks. She squeezes my hand. Somehow, her hand is now holding mine. "Look at me."

Reluctantly, with tears rolling down my cheeks, I gaze up at her. She's holding up her shirt. A web of scars peeks out above the waistband of her sweatpants—a tangle of lace-like flesh that wraps clear around her hip. I glance from this up to her face and see that she's looking at my own exposed stomach. I look back at her wound. I'm the asshole. I'm the guy who thinks he's uniquely miserable, who thinks all the world's woes are his, who sees the pure in everyone else and the dilapidated within. Only I have suffered. Only I know pain. How do you share what you think no one else can hold? Why do we all do this to ourselves and each other? Why can't we just fucking cry like men?

I do in that moment. Gone is the allure of having sex with this woman. Gone is the allure of loving her and spending the rest of my life with her. Gone are all the good things I dream about. All that's left is the awful, the horrendous, the brutal, and the hurt.

The last bit of egoism I have left in me is to think to myself—as I convulse with sobs and bawl like a child—that no one has ever cried like this. It's the last time I'll ever think I'm unique. The last time. Because as soon as I think that no one has ever cried like this, a woman is wrapping herself around me, a stranger, a sister, a fellow wounded, a lonely lover. And she shows me that I'm not alone. And we cry like the universe is about to end.

25
CHAPTER

There's something oddly familiar about the way she strokes my hair after, the way she looks at me, the way her hair is mussed and her cheeks are flushed. She must be thinking the same thing, because the first thing either of us says in what feels like forever is her asking:

"Was it good for you?"

We both laugh. It's the best kind of laughter. "What the hell *was* that?" I ask. Because nothing happened other than the holding and crying.

"That's called feeling something, soldier. Good to see you can still do it."

There's something scarily clinical about the way she says this. She tucks my hair behind my ear. Definitely not reg length. And I can't stop myself from thinking that maybe she was sent here to tune more than that other beacon. That's paranoia, though. That's remnants of my ego. A billion stars staring at me from across the unfathomable distance, and it's not the cosmos that teaches me how small I am. It's this perfect person lifting her shirt and reminding me that no one's perfect. We all have stories. And regrets. And weaknesses. She pulled off what astronomy couldn't. Or maybe it was just about damn time for me.

"I don't want you to leave," I say.

She nods. "I know."

Cricket growls in her sleep. The warthen passed out as soon as we were done bawling, like it had exhausted her as well. I reckon that, if she's really an empath, it did.

"Are you glad you met me?" Claire asks.

"Of course." There's no hesitation.

"There you go," she says.

I rub her arm. I memorize how she feels for later. I take her free hand and pull it to my lips, kiss the back of her hand, feel her squeeze my hand in assent, then take a deep sniff, trying to memorize how she smells.

"Have you ever done this before?" I ask.

Claire laughs. "Would it matter?"

I shrug.

A moment passes.

"No," she says. "I probably needed this more than you did."

The old me would've privately doubted. The new me isn't so sure. Maybe her path has been harder than mine. Maybe I can let go of the specialness of my suffering. Maybe the handholds I've been clinging to have been digging into my palm and cutting me rather than keeping me from falling.

"If you ever want to share," I say. "I'm here." Because I can be the shoulder too. I can listen instead of not-talking.

I can prop someone else up. Me. The broken one. No: *a* broken one.

I think of Tex, a grizzled vet who served in my last squad, who died the day I won my medal. I always thought Tex was crazy. He was the happiest motherfucker you ever met. And not happy with the zeal of killing, which a few of the really off-kilter vets got, but happy with the joy of being alive that day and wanting to remain that way for one more day. Tex would introduce himself to every goo-green kid who joined the squad, every piece of farm-fresh. He'd put his arm around their shoulder, tell them his life story, his real name, ask them all about their hometowns, so that even those nearby had to learn shit we'd rather not. We'd get hit by these frag grenades of nicety. He took people in, Tex. Got close to them. Cried like a baby when the smoke cleared and the tags were tallied. And I thought he was fucking crazy, going about war like that. Not learning what the rest of us learned.

But he may have been the only sane one. The human out there with all us aliens. Still living. Refusing to give up. Preferring to yo-yo up and down like grav panels on the fritz. Preferring that to the weightlessness. To the lack of gravity.

I want to feel a little numb again. I smile at Claire. "You want to go sit up at the gwib with me? Just for a little bit?"

A frown shatters her beautiful face. She looks sad again, but not the raw sadness of all those wounds in her life—this is sadness mixed with pity. This is her not wanting to tell me some awful truth.

"You know it doesn't do anything, right?" she says.

No. I don't know. I have no idea what she means.

"The gwib. There's no way it interacts with your brain."

"Fuck that," I tell her. "Yes it does. It mellows me out. It's the only thing that does—"

She brushes her hand across my cheek, and I feel something else that mellows me. I was getting worked up just then, but her touch calms me down. I know I'm right, and she's wrong, but I don't need to get upset about it. Just accept.

"You feel calm up there because it's the only place you sit still," she says. "It's where you breathe. Where you let yourself relax. You can do that anywhere. You just have to choose. Just *be*."

I shake my head. I'm about to argue with her, when she runs her hand down my cheek, down my neck, and touches the rock hanging from its lanyard.

"What's this?"

I place my hand on the back of hers. I think of Scarlett for a moment, how sex and love used to mean the same thing. But this is love, what I'm feeling right now. The surest I've ever felt it. Romantic or not. Just human to human. Real love.

"A memento," I say.

"What does it remind you of?"

I think about this. So many answers. I want to make sure I choose the honest one.

"That I'm not always right," I finally say. "It reminds me to question myself. Question everything. And never stop."

Claire smiles. She touches my lips with her finger, then leans in and kisses me. When she pulls back, much too soon, she says, "Well, you got that part right. Never question that. Hold on to it."

I pull her against me, not to make love to her, but just to love her. To hold something good and imperfect and fucked up, and to feel someone holding all of that in return.

CHAPTER ②⑥

It's moving day. I watch on the zoomed-in vid screen as the supply shuttle makes its approach to beacon 1529, little puffs of uncertainty as the pilot tries to line up with the lock collar. On the HF, I hear him proclaim contact and good hold. They must give these back-sector routes to the greenest fliers. I shudder to think my precious Claire is entrusting her life to this noob.

"Gotcha," I hear her radio back. That voice. We spent hours the last few nights chatting via the HF, after having spent hours chatting in person, and saying we should really get back to our own beacons, and then saying we should really get off the radio and get some sleep, and then waking up and making up an excuse to see each other again.

When Claire caught me unplugging the CO_2 sensor alarm in her life support module—and I fessed up to three other things I'd broken over there that might be serious enough to keep her around, fixing stuff, but not so serious that anything would happen to her—she got a strange look on her face, like she knew this was going too far, and we were feeling too much, even though we still hadn't had sex, like we were saving that for the people we didn't love quite so truly. Well, it was after this that she QTed NASA and said the beacon was good to go. To send her an operator. At least, I think this was what decided it for her.

Cricket mews and growls and nudges her head against me.

"I know," I say, scratching behind her ears. "I like her too."

The warthen clamps her jaw on my arm and squeezes, like she'll bite me if I don't stop lying.

"Love," I say quickly. "I love her. Okay? But I'm supposed to tell *her* that, not you. So leave me the hell alone about it."

Cricket pulls away and walks a big lap around the command module, whining.

"I'm sorry," I say, throwing my hands up. "Whaddya want from me? Huh? I don't make the rules. I just break them. Can't it be enough that we had a good week? Does it have to be all about today?"

Cricket stares at me. I can hear that I'm asking myself these questions. That it's me angry at the cosmos.

"C'mere," I say, patting my lap.

Fifty kilos of alien jumps up in my lap and finds a way to curl into a dense, furry ball. Her tail swishes along the ground, back and forth.

"Truth is, I'm scared," I tell her. "What if sitting still stops working? Or breathing in and out doesn't do anything anymore? If the gwib doesn't do anything, what if everything else stops working too?"

She licks my hand. And then I have a scary thought, one I shove away fast before Cricket can pick up on it—and the question is this: What if I were to lose her right now? This animal is the nearest thing I have to the GWB, or Rocky, or Claire, or all the things that have given me peace in the moment but never seem to last. Where's the everlasting peace? Is there even such a thing? Or do we war like alien races war, eternally, against ourselves? I hope that's not right. I hope that's not how it all works.

"Beacon 23, transport KYM731. Requesting permission to dock. Over."

I look back to my screen and see that the supply ship has left its collar. It's just the lifeboat there. There are lights in the portholes and flashing lights along the solar panels. She's all up and running.

"Hop down," I tell Cricket.

She does, and I grab the HF's mic.

"Lock collar Charlie," I say, reaching over to energize the magnetic latch.

I go down the ladder ahead of Cricket and close the ladder's top hatch behind me. I can hear her pacing and mewing, but she doesn't put up a big fight. Maybe she can read my thoughts and knows that if she gets spotted here, I'll lose her, and she'll probably spend the rest of her life in a zoo. Or get bought up by another bounty hunter, who'll use her with his dark thoughts.

The pilot whaps the collar pretty damn good. A one out of ten on the pilot-o-meter. I key open the airlock, and we shake hands and exchange names and pleasantries. Then he passes me two dozen plastic crates full of supplies, spares, and food, and I pass him back two canisters of unrecyclable waste. He gives me two empties in exchange. The entire time, I keep expecting Claire to come give us a hand, or say one last goodbye, or at least wave. But the last time we saw each other, it was too perfect a final goodbye to replace. A lingering kiss that I can still feel on my lips. A warmness in my heart that liquor and grav wave broadcasters could never touch.

"One last thing," the pilot says. He disappears and comes back with a black plastic bag. The top is seized with a red wire. A tear rolls down my cheek, and I don't turn aside, and I don't wipe it away. I don't even feel the pride of someone who does neither. Nor the pride of not feeling this. Instead, I just am. I feel the sweetness of the gift. I feel the sweetness of feeling the sweetness. There's no shame, just a distant awareness that something in me has changed.

"Can never have too much of this," I say.

The pilot is looking at me funny. I untwist the wire and pull out the can of WD-80, then make a show of appraising it. "It's a good year." It's been a good week, at least.

"Yeah, whatever," the pilot says. "The operator just told me to give that to you. I swear you people are strange."

He turns and heads back through the airlock.

"Tuner," I shout after him. "She's a tuner."

He looks back at me.

"You think she looks like an operator?" I ask.

He shrugs. And then, reaching to key his door shut, he says, "You all look the same to me."

"Wait!" I say. I peer past him into the supply ship, which brings us our food and our spares and the people who replace us, and which takes us home if we ever decide to go. I search for some sign of her, but there is none.

"Yeah?"

I show him the can of lubricant. One quick burst, and things just slide together. "Thank her for me," I say. "Just tell her I appreciate it."

Another look like I'm the crazy one.

"Tell her yourself," he says. "She's your neighbor. I'm outta here."

•••

It takes me three or four stunned breaths to put it all together. And then I take the three ladders quicker than I ever have. If there were an Olympic event for beacon operators, I would've set the galactic record. It never would've been broken again. That is, until I hit the hatch that leads into the command module.

I free the clamps holding the hatch and give it a shove, but the thing won't budge.

"Cricket!" I yell. "MOVE! Cricket! Off—!" I grunt with effort, climb another rung and put my shoulder to the hatch. I feel it rise a centimeter or two, but then it collapses back down as Cricket shifts her weight.

"I swear, Cricket, get the hell off! I'm trying to get up there. Bad girl! Move!"

Finally I get it lifted enough that she slides off. She jumps out of the way as the hatch falls into its recessed slot in the deck. Then Cricket's all over me as I try to get up the last rungs of the ladder, licking me with her rough tongue.

"For fuck's sake," I tell her. "Cricket. C'mon. Leave it. No licking. Never lick me again. I swear."

I'm grumbling at her as I get to the HF and pick up the mic. I squeeze the transmit button, then let go. I nearly said something. Switching to the lock bay's external camera, I watch the supply ship pull away. *No she didn't,* I tell myself. *No she didn't. No she didn't. She wouldn't. She wouldn't.*

I try to talk myself down as I wait for the supply ship to get the hell into hyperspace. I try to picture some bald man with a beer gut over on that other beacon, scratching his neck, chewing on a protein pack. That's the truth. Hold on to that. Don't get your hopes up.

The supply ship ramps up its drive and vanishes from my screen.

I squeeze the mic.

"Beacon 1529? This is beacon 23. You read me? Over."

I wait.

There's no response.

I switch my scanner back to get a visual on the beacon.

The lifeboat is still there. Still attached.

"Go ahead."

The words are clipped. Came when I wasn't paying attention. But it was her. I'm pretty sure it was her. Pretty sure.

"Claire?" I ask.

"Go ahead," she answers.

I take a deep breath. I steady myself with one hand on the dash. Cricket is there, leaning against me. She puts her mouth on my arm and squeezes, threatening to bite me if I make the wrong move.

"I know," I tell Cricket. "We both do."

And I can't remember the last time I said the words and meant them like this. Can't remember the last time.

But I'll always remember this one.

⑤

VISITOR

CHAPTER

(27)

I hated Sundays as a kid. From the moment I woke up, I could feel Monday looming, could feel another school week all piled up and ready to smother me. How was I supposed to enjoy a day of freedom while drowning in dread like that? It was impossible. A pit would form in my chest and gut—this indescribable emptiness that I knew should be filled with fun, but instead left me casting about for something to do.

Knowing I should be having fun was a huge part of the problem. Knowing that this was a rare day off, a welcome reprieve, and here I was miserable and fighting against it. Maybe this was why Fridays at school were better than Sundays *not* in school. I was happier doing what I hated, knowing a Saturday was coming, than I was on a perfectly free Sunday with a Monday right around the corner.

I call this the Relativistic Weekend Effect. We live in the present, but our happiness relies heavily on the future. Our mood is as much expectation as experience. Just like in the army, where life in the trenches worked the same way. It was the quiet that jangled the nerves. It was the lead-up before the push more than the push itself. To this day, I grow more faint at the scent of gun oil than I do at the sight of blood.

Maybe this is why it feels like a waking nightmare, living the galactic dream. I've got it all. I've got my own place[1], a steady girlfriend[2], a loving pet[3], a decent-paying job[4], a reliable car[5], peace and privacy[6], and the best view of the galactic core that doesn't require a lead vest[7].

Yup, I'm truly living the dream.

So why do I feel like someone is about to pinch me?

•••

Merchants and pirates pass through my sector now and then and leave behind trade goods and news of the war. Everything's changing. The items I now barter for betray the fact that I'm in a relationship with the girl next door. I score flowers, a wedge of cheese, and two small blocks of chocolate from a gentleman I'll call a "merchant" if he'll promise not to laugh. I also learn from him of the first

---

1 A junked-up nav beacon on the edge of sector eight.

2 She's dreamy.

3 Okay, sometimes I think she wants to kill me. She's like a cross between a Labrador and a leopard. And I'm pretty sure she reads minds.

4 Honestly, I can't tell why I'm even needed here.

5 If you can call a NASA lifeboat a "car." It gets me to my girl's place and back. Drives like shit.

6 In deep space, no one can hear you sob.

7 Look at all that nothingness. Can you feel it looking back?

battle in sector eight, a small skirmish a couple light years along this arm of the Milky Way. I can imagine how it went down, having been in more than a few dogfights myself. A Ryph scout cruiser meets an exploratory force that has broken off from the main fleet. Shots are fired. One of the small navy ships goes down. Just another casualty of a war that's taken billions on either side.

But then some cleric in the navy's offices back at Sol logs the coordinates and notifies the kid's parents of the last known location of their son's or daughter's atoms. And that cleric or that parent or some intrepid reporter notices that *technically,* the ship was just over some arbitrary line and that *technically,* the war has now moved into sector eight, and that *technically,* this means the galaxy proper is now well and truly fucked.

Talking heads blather across the holosphere. Young men and women gather outside recruiting centers, chests thrust out, to sign their noble death certificates. Thirty-two settled and semi-settled worlds across sector eight tremble. Sectors two and three start voting out doves and voting in hawks. Everyone on Earth wonders when sector one will get their turn. All the other sectors wonder the same goddamn thing.

Meanwhile, the Ryph advance. Meanwhile, war gets closer. There's no stopping it.

These are my pleasant and cheery thoughts as I drive chocolate and flowers over to the neighboring beacon for a date. It's Sunday out on the edge of sector eight. A day of rest. But I don't know how anyone can.

28

CHAPTER

It's been so long since I've dated that I can't remember exactly how. But Claire is a patient teacher. She's already reminded me how to cry in the company of another, and that's a big thing to learn. As a boy growing up in Tennessee, you learned never to cry where anyone else could see. Crying was a sign of weakness. When we were kids, tears made the other boys around us brave.

In the army, it was different. You still went off and found a place to cry alone, but you weren't scared of your brothers and sisters in arms. In the army, tears made everyone else afraid. You didn't want to spread the weakness. Tears are contagious things.

I saw my father cry once and only once. It wasn't when I left for war, and it wasn't when Mom died. It wasn't when my brother got out of rehab and we both saw that look in his eyes and knew he'd never drink again. It wasn't when our sister married an officer from Cyphus and we knew we'd be lucky to see her every other holiday. Those were all times when I felt like I might explode, keeping my grief or relief all locked up. Those were times that sent me off to my room, alone, to weep into my palms.

But not my dad. No, the only day I saw him bawl was the day he pushed in the clutch on the old tractor, and the brake lines were dry, and the tractor lurched backward down the hill before he could get it in gear again, and there was just a muffled yip from our dog, who always followed too close to that tractor, and then she was gone.

I never asked Dad why it was that time. This was after Mom was gone, and Shelly was on Cyphus, and Tyrese was clean, and I'd already enlisted and finished boot camp. This was after all of that. But there he was, clutching his dog, who was already old and had lived the kind of long and leisurely life that any dog in the galaxy would dream of, whose coat had grown white and whose eyes had gone rheumy, and who hadn't suffered a bit—had just gone out doing the happy thing she loved best: following my dad around the property.

I watched my father cry for half an hour. This was two days before I deployed. I came to his side, and I stood there, feeling more shocked and confused than sad. I mean, I loved the dog, but I loved my dad more, and I didn't know what the hell to do to comfort him. The navy had just taught me how to pull a Star Swift out of a flat spin in atmo and get her back into orbit, but no one had taught me how to put my arm around my bawling father. No one.

I retreated to the porch and watched from there. After a while, I felt angry. He never cried for me like that, not once. Not for Mom. Not for Shelly. Not for Tyrese.

I think I've held on to that anger for too long. Never understood what my father was crying about. Not until Claire told me it was okay to let go, and when I did, I found myself crying for everything. And everyone. And even myself a little.

I wish I had known what my dad was going through that day. I hated him for crying about the wrong things. But I get it now that he was crying for *everything*. He was crying for me. Crying because I was going off to war. Because the chances were better than even that he'd never see me again.

I guess those dry brake lines broke more than his pup's back that day. Whatever was still holding my father together snapped as well. I've felt that. It's something deep in the chest that goes. A rupture between the part of us that pulses and the part of us that breathes. To hold that together, you need an embrace from someone who cares. My father needed that embrace. He needed it that day, rather than the perfunctory and chickenshit one I gave him on my day of deployment. The day his pup died was the true day I went off to war. It was the day my father really needed me. And I sat on the porch and was angry at the world.

This is the story of my life, I suppose: always in the right place at the right time, and then I don't do anything. I stand there. Or I rock back and forth in my grandfather's chair. Or I go find a place along the trenches where it's nice and quiet, and I fill that place with hot tears.

So this is the thing I learned from Claire: Crying isn't simply about opening the floodgates to some private trauma and letting it out—crying is just as much about letting those around you know you're hurting. Our tears are trying to serve a purpose, but we rarely let them. I don't know how we got started with subverting that purpose— maybe it starts with bullies in middle school, or parents telling their kids not to cry 'cause it embarrasses them in public—I just know that it takes a bit of courage to unlearn that shame, and to be there for others when they try to unlearn that shame, and that it all gets easier after you feel how healthy it is.

Beacon 1529 fills my lifeboat's canopy while I muse on these things. I swing to the side and dock up to the magnetic collar that leads to the airlock. It's a ten out of ten on the pilot-o-meter. When I pop the hatch, Cricket goes bounding inside, looking for Claire, who shouts down from the life support module to come on up. NASA did not build these ladders with boyfriends holding flowers and chocolate and cheese in mind. I climb with my elbows and even employ my chin once or twice. Above me, Cricket's tail happily *thwump-thwump*s against the pumps and gensets and machinery that fill the cramped module.

"Honey, I'm home!" I call.

This is something I've heard people say in holocoms. Claire laughs every time. Almost like she can imagine the two of us sharing a home together. A normal life. Planetside. As soon as I get my head above the grating, Cricket turns and licks my face. If my warthen can read minds like I think she can, she has to know how much I hate this. And yet she does it anyway. Maybe she hates me. Maybe that's why she does it.

"No," I tell her, warding her off with lilies, appledots, butterflaps, and three other alien varietals not listed in the archives. Cricket turns in excited circles while I hand the flowers to Claire. One of the appledots is broken and leans over like it's given up on life.

"For me?" Claire asks. She wipes the sweat from her brow and takes the flowers, sniffs them, tries to straighten the stricken appledot.

"Yeah, and I don't think any are toxic," I say.

She leans in to kiss me. Her lips taste of salt and grease. "They're beautiful. And your beacon is officially under the worst quarantine in the history of quarantines. Why don't you take these back to the lifeboat? The last thing I need is mites getting loose in here. Or roaches."

"The trader said they were clean," I protest.

Claire shoots me a look. I show her the chocolate and the cheese. The look persists. Like I said, I'm not very good at this whole dating thing.

"Should I put Cricket out the airlock as well?" I ask. "She might have fleas."

Cricket growls at me. Claire scratches the alien behind the ears and gives me that look I used to see on my CO when he gave orders that he knew contradicted both reason and his last set of orders. "Whatever damage sweet Cricket has done has been done," she says.

Cricket turns and cocks her head at this, like she can't imagine ever doing an ounce of damage. I leave them both and put the flowers and the rest of the contraband back in the lifeboat. When I return, Claire is wiping her hands on a rag and putting her tools away. I give her another kiss before heading up to the galley to put dinner together.

Our days are a lot like this, all the little boring bits in the holocoms between the laugh tracks. There's a lot of anticipation that something is going to happen, something really funny or tragic, but it rarely ever does. It rarely ever does, but you can still feel it coming.

29

CHAPTER

"On or off?" Claire asks.

It's after dinner, and Claire and I are up by the gravity wave broadcaster, which is the business end of the nav beacon. I sit still and concentrate before I answer. How am I feeling? Stressed out? Depressed? Mellow? Content? I want to get it right. I'm trying to prove a point here. I've been trying to prove it for over a week.

I rest my head against the dome of the GWB, which has always relaxed me in the past. I'm supposed to guess if Claire has the power to the dome on or off (and yeah, we only do this when there's no traffic passing through). She keeps the results tallied, won't tell me how I've fared thus far, doesn't want me to have any feedback. Claire contends that I'm imagining the effects of the GWB on my brain, says she doesn't feel anything when she sits in the same spot. But I know I do.

"The power is . . . on," I say, giving her my answer. "I think. I'm pretty sure."

"How sure?" She makes a note on her tablet.

"It's . . . there are confounding variables."

"Like?"

"You," I tell her. And it's true. Just being around her, I can feel my pulse race less, my breathing grow deeper and more relaxed, my limbs feel free of the trembles and shakes.

Claire leans over and kisses my cheek. "I think that's enough for today," she says.

"So how'd I do?"

She laughs at me for asking. Like I should know better. Cricket burrows her head into my hand, reminding me that I've stopped scratching her. I resume. "I swear I can feel the difference," I say. "I can tell when it's on. It feels so soothing."

Claire puts the tablet away. She takes a deep breath, like she's contemplating something. Then she turns to me, her guise suddenly serious. "I believe you," she says. "I do. I'm starting to believe you. I'm just curious if it's really the GWB or something else."

"Like . . . you think it's all in my head?" I touch the rock dangling from my neck. Ever since that cargo out of Orion splashed into a trillion pieces across my asteroid field, I've had a pretty loose grip on reality. Looser than normal, I guess I should say.

"I don't know." Claire bites her lower lip. "I guess I just know the spectrum the gwib works on, and they've been tested like hell to make sure they don't have any biological effects, otherwise we wouldn't let you all come up here while they're running and even get *close* to them—"

"Maybe there's something wrong with *me*," I say.

Claire nods. "Maybe." Somehow she misses the very loud and obvious cast from my rod as I go fishing for a compliment, or for reassurances. Or hell—I'd be happy with a little bit of a pause before acknowledging that, indeed, there might be something wrong with my head.

And then it hits me like a frag grenade with its fuse delay set to max. I finally get that she's sharing with me the results of our tests, that she's admitting I've been getting them mostly right.

"So I've been scoring pretty good?" I ask. Otherwise, why would she be worried about me?

Claire bites her lip.

"How good? Have I gotten many wrong?"

Claire glances at her tablet. She's back to biting her lip. There's no way she'd worry something was wrong with me unless I'm nailing it better than chance would dictate. Something statistically significant. I reach for the tablet. "Can I see? Please. C'mon, Claire."

And she can see that it's important to me. Cricket licks my arm as I lean over and take the tablet from her. Claire lets it go. There's a spreadsheet on the screen. I scroll up, seeing all the check marks from our past dinner dates, and it takes a moment to see where the Xs would even go. Because there aren't any. I've been right every time.

I feel an immense sense of relief. I might be crazy, but I wasn't wrong. I've always known the GWB messes with my head, and I've always assumed it messes with everyone's head, but Claire really had me going there for a while. She really had me thinking it was just the act of sitting quietly and *thinking* it was working that was calming me.

"Maybe it's something you came into contact with in the trenches. A toxin, perhaps—"

I nod, thinking this is likely. Lord knows, I've sucked in enough alien atmo and bioblasts. No telling what's been in my lungs. I never got Nile teeth syndrome or the blue cough like a lot of soldiers, but perhaps I got something the docs missed.

"Or maybe it's neurological," Claire offers. She's puzzling through this the way she tunes beacons, getting them ready for service. Looking back at the tablet in my hand—which she uses to get these nav beacons sorted—I wonder how much of my appeal to her is that I'm broken. I wonder what she's doing here. Why she stayed. How NASA would've allowed a tuner to become an operator.

"Neurological how?" I ask.

"Well, it's just that . . . maybe it's more of an experienced trauma, rather than a foreign body. You have all the signs of . . . you know—"

"Trench rot," I say. "Blast shock. War weariness. Soldier syndrome—"

"Post traumatic stress disorder," Claire says, opting for the clinical rather than the descriptive. Lots of dirty truths hide in those clean syllables.

"What would that have to do with this?"

Claire shrugs. "I probably know as much about how the gwibs work as the people who invented them, and nothing I know accounts for why you would feel anything from what they do."

"Should I be worried?" I feel like I should be worried. Claire is a whole lot smarter than me, and she looks worried. She places her hand on my arm, and I see a brave smile on her face, the one she keeps plastered over her concern for me.

"Everything's going to be fine," she says. "We'll figure this out, you and me. Everything's going to be perfectly fine."

But I know she's wrong. I heard it from the man who sold me the flowers and the chocolate and the cheese. I know something bad is coming. I know it's near. There are rumors of two fleets amassing on either side of this galactic arm, rumors of the navy collecting all its ships, and of the Ryph stockpiling all *their* ships, and no one knows whether these rumors are true, but we tend to spread and believe the worst of what we hear. It's so much easier to believe the worst.

I don't know what I believe. I've learned to doubt my mind. I need evidence. Facts. Like the sound from the proximity alarm, which begins to emit its soft blare, which in Claire's beacon sounds similar to the old air raid sirens the army uses. We have a visitor. And it's no great coincidence that bad things arrive while I'm thinking about them. No coincidence at all. Because I've been thinking about this for over a year now. I've known that this was coming for longer than I've worked here in sector eight. I've known it because there's no escaping it. War is always coming—it's only ever a matter of time. And right now, beyond our porthole, the time comes.

CHAPTER 30

Almost as soon as the ships arrive, one of them is destroyed. It happens so fast, I assume at first that it's an impact death, that some ship not on our schedule tried to pass through here at twenty times the speed of light and met a disastrous end among the asteroids. There's even a twinge of guilt that maybe Claire's beacon was down for our little experiment—except that I'd sensed the beacon was on, and my beacon is also up and running, so it can't be that.

This and more spins through my mind in the handful of moments it takes for all the combustibles aboard the ship to glow and expand in an orange ball and then fall perfectly still.

What's left is a Ryph Reaper, one of the bigger enemy cruisers, its forward-swept arms studded with laser pods and missile hardpoints. The terror of the cosmos. The only ship that ever got the best of me. The shit of nightmares. *My* nightmares.

Cricket bolts from my lap. The warthen growls and swipes at the porthole with her claws. Claire's hand is digging into my arm. We are otherwise frozen, watching as the ship remains in view through the porthole. Remains in view because it's coming straight for us.

"Go, go," I say, trying not to yell, trying to remain calm. I only got a glimpse of the ship that went nova, but it looked like a Navy Talon. Must've been a pursuit through hyperspace for them to come out on top of each other like that. The war is here. It's really goddamn *here*. And we're sitting ducks. No—we're fish in a NASA-white barrel.

Claire launches herself down the chute toward the command module. I make Cricket go in front of me, watching her tail swish the weightlessness and her paws swipe at the walls until she reaches gravity on the other side. I'm right behind them.

"Lifeboat," Claire says, rushing for the ladder.

I run to the QT and send a quick message to NASA: *undr attck*. I leave out the vowels because we don't have time, not because of regs. Then I chase after Claire, wondering how either of our lifeboats is better than the beacon. We don't have a ship that can outrun a Reaper. I listen for the proximity alarm to signal more of our incoming fleet. Or their incoming fleet. The only thing that can save us is for the navy to get here. How are they not here?

We take the ladders as fast as we can. The temptation to run to a porthole and get a visual on the Reaper is overwhelming. Without being able to see where it is, there's a dread that our lives could end at any minute—a flash of plasma, and then our atoms are mingling in the void.

Another ladder. Claire's living quarters. The bed where we first made love. A handful of my things. Some clothes I keep over here, neatly folded next to hers. A swirl and dent in the middle of the bed made by Cricket. All these signs of a comfortable, happy life flash by in my peripheral. Things I'll never see again. Things I'll never feel again. I'm back at the front. Back in the trenches. Thinking about home. Aching to go home.

I follow Cricket down the next ladder, taking in a slide what she spans in a leap. No weapon, no attack craft, no way of defending ourselves. But I'm forming a plan, one of those desperate plans, some way of making sure Claire and Cricket get out of here alive.

Before I take the next ladder, I grab the largest of the adjustable wrenches from the tool locker. I take the last ladder more slowly, one hand on the rungs, the other handling the heft of the tool. I jump down the last five rungs. Claire is in her beacon's lifeboat, yelling for me to get in. Cricket is standing in the airlock, looking at me over her shoulder, tail tucked between her legs, feeling our fear. All she knows is that her human companions are deathly afraid.

"In," I say, waving at Cricket.

She hesitates. She knows what I'm thinking.

I shove at Cricket's rump. "Let's go," I tell her. I imagine myself getting in the lifeboat as well. I try to believe it. So Cricket will believe it.

With me pushing and Claire tugging, we get Cricket through the airlock and into the lifeboat. I don't even think to lean in for a last kiss. Too much racing through my head. Too many days of standing in an airlock just like this and thinking similar fates but never with so noble a purpose. I key the lifeboat's outer door shut, then my airlock door, and then I disengage the ship from the lock collar. Wielding the adjustable wrench like a baseball bat, I take a mean swing at the control panel. There's a crunch, and the hiss, sparkle, and smell of an electrical short. I catch a glimpse of Claire staring at me through the porthole as the lifeboat begins to drift away.

Dropping the wrench, I run for my lifeboat. I know sound can't travel through a vacuum. I know this. I know my pet and my lover—my two best friends in the cosmos—are drifting away. But I swear I can hear Cricket's howling lament. I swear I can hear Claire asking me what in the hell I'm thinking. My warthen is an empath, so I can understand hearing her voice. As for Claire's, it wouldn't be the first time under duress that I started imagining things.

•••

At the helm of my lifeboat, I release from the beacon and pivot to scan the area. Reaching overhead, I flip the radio on. "Claire, you there?"

"I'm here. What the fuck are you doing?"

Her voice is a blast of static and anger. I hear the soldier in her, not the nav beacon tuner. Hard to believe what we once were and what we are now.

"Listen closely," I say. I'm watching the Reaper approach. It's still heading for the beacon. I engage the thrust and race out toward it. "I want you to head toward the nearest big asteroid you can find. Grab hold of it with the pinchers and shut your boat down. Wait for the navy. Stay off the radio. Do you read?"

"What're you doing?" Claire asks. And I realize that's not static behind her voice. It's Cricket. Hissing and growling.

"Go now," I tell her. "Before any more of the Ryph get here. Please. Just go."

Tears stream down my cheeks at the thought of anything happening to her or Cricket. The attack ship adjusts course toward the lifeboats. I don't have the thrusters or control jets to outmaneuver it. I don't have any weapon other than my desperation. I keep a steady hand on the control stick, ready to dodge incoming fire, but the enemy ship knows I'm no threat. It just races onward. I race to intercept. On my scanner, I can see that Claire has her boat going at full tilt as well. She's heading toward the rocks. A good soldier. Can see there's no stopping me, and that this isn't going to be a holo where the hero and the girl profess their love while the bad guys wait patiently to make it a climactic finale. This isn't going to be a holo where anyone has time to sit, frozen in place. This isn't even going to be a holo with a hero. Just two people in the wrong place at the wrong time.

I adjust course to make it look like I'm trying to slide by the Reaper and escape. It's all about giving Claire time. An extra target. I know what the Ryph are here to do; I've been on these runs from the other side. They'll take out one of the beacons and rig the other to blow. Or rig them both to blow. But they'll hold at least one so they control this airspace. It's the same tactic used in the old wars when bridges were both lusted after and strung with blast charges. No way through this sector without a beacon. The Ryph must've cracked our GWB frequency, just like we cracked theirs. I'm thinking like a soldier, piloting like a flyboy, forming tactics like a man in love.

The Reaper races my way. No shots fired yet. Claire is halfway to the asteroid field. Moments before we pass, I throw my ship to the side, attempting to ram the Reaper. The Ryph pilot is fast; he flits to the side and out of the way, but I'm spinning sideways, rotating as I barrel forward, and I extend the sampling arm tucked under the nose of the boat, reaching out, making my craft as long as possible, just want to touch, to make contact at full speed, to let this beast know that I pose a threat, for him to concentrate on me—

There's a clang as the sampling arm hits the Reaper's trailing wing. A racket. I slam against the side canopy, the crappy NASA restraints giving way, not meant for this. Stars flash in my vision. And then a hiss. An alarm as the cabin begins to lose pressure. Cold leaks in. A hull rupture. The constellations become a blur as the lifeboat spins in space, and I have one brief moment of lucidity left in which to wonder if I did more damage to my enemy than to myself. Just that angry hope before a bulkhead gives way in my lifeboat, and all that pressurized air rushes out, taking me with it.

As I cartwheel through the ruptured hull and out among the lonely and quiet stars, my lungs begin to burn. They say you can survive in the cold vacuum of space for nearly a minute if you hold your breath. Icy tears glaze my vision, and I wonder why anyone would even bother.

(31) CHAPTER

Every morning is an afterlife. Every evening, I die anew in the trenches amid nightmares of artillery finding their target. To wake each morning is a surprise. To rise a miracle. To breathe another breath some gift foisted upon me and beyond my control.

My eyes flutter open and settle on an old man standing before a lighthouse, a great wave crashing all around him. I know what that feels like. The man seems unaware of what's coming, but I think maybe he knows. I think maybe he's numb to it all. I don't think that's ignorance on his bearded and weathered face; I believe that's resignation.

A Ryph Lord moves before me and blocks the view of the picture. They say I'm one of the few who have ever been this close to a Lord and lived to tell the tale. Here I am again. Life appears to be full of coincidences like this, until you learn how it all pieces together.

"You're awake," someone says.

I recognize the voice. It's Rocky. I try to lift my arms to touch the rock on its lanyard, this little piece of asteroid that I found among the debris of the wrecked cargo, but my arms are bound. I look down at my wrists, seized together and tied to my knees, which are bound together as well. I can't move.

The Ryph Lord hovers over me. My throat burns, maybe from dying out there among the stars. I try to focus my thoughts on Claire and Cricket, knowing I should remember something, a vision coalescing of them heading for safety, but I can't remember if they made it. All I care about in that moment is whether they're alive. I want my navy to come and rescue them. I lock down on this thought, trying to ignore the voices of my insanity. I try to see my love and my beloved animal safe and in some faraway place, some place where war will never reach—

"Yo, asshole, I'm talking to you."

"Shaddup, Rocky."

My voice is a rasp. I should be dead. I wish I were dead. I should've been dead a thousand times over. Unable to move, I feel my heart racing, despite my head being so close to the GWB. So it's not the sitting still that calms; it's the sitting still *voluntarily*. A soul can't be pinned and made to heal. It has to be talked into stillness and quietude. It has to want it.

"I'd say this is rather important," Rocky says. His voice seems to float up from my necklace, but I know it's all in my head. I hear voices in my dreams. Don't we all? Our brains can fool us. Mine makes a fool out of me.

The Ryph Lord shifts his great bulk from one leg to the other. The Ryph are bipedal, like all the sentient races we know, with skin like a shark's beneath their flight and combat suits. A face split by a vertical rift reveals rows of sharp teeth. Eyes lie to either side, and they bore into my skull. Two three-clawed hands are balled into fists. Muscles like steel. The biggest and baddest of the Ryph, Lords are never taken alive, rarely taken whole. I don't understand what this one is waiting for. Kill me, already. Or untie me so I can do it myself.

"Stop ignoring me," my pet rock says.

"Not now, Rocky."

"Yeah right, not now. Like I'm happy with any of this. I need this guy looking at us like I needed the hole you put in my head. And hey, what was up with that?"

"You aren't real."

"Let's table that. This guy has a favor he wants to ask. So open your ears and give a listen. Give a listen, and I'll shut up."

I stare at the Ryph Lord. My mind is clearing a little. It occurs to me that every moment delayed like this is good for Claire, Cricket, and the navy. Maybe my death can be put off for a moment or two. Maybe these last few minutes can serve some larger purpose.

"I'm listening," I say.

"Listen harder," Rocky tells me.

I wait. I can feel a thrum in the deck from distant machinery somewhere in the beacon. I can hear the whirring of a pump way down in the living modules. I can hear Rocky breathing, as if rocks can do such a thing. And then I hear the whisper, a hoarse voice launched across the cosmos like a dandelion seed on a breeze, a hiss beyond the vacuum, a single word below the senses, too dull to register, coming like an ache in my bones, like neutrinos dancing across the surface of my skull—

hello

It is fainter than my imaginary voices, and yet somehow more real. Able to be believed. I hear Rocky holding his breath. I feel the welcomed numbness of the GWB leach into my mood.

"Hello," I whisper back, the word held in my mouth, uttered inside my throat, not passing between my lips. A word of thought.

remember me

It's not a question but a command. A desperate plea. Like how the dead wish to be remembered. Like great-great-grandfathers would have others know their names. Not the war heroes with the medals, but the obscure, those who didn't fight. Those who died quietly with loved ones around and who were lowered into fathom-deep trenches rather than scraped out of kilometer-long ones.

The Ryph Lord moves, comes at me with his fist uncurled, those fearsome claws sharp as razors, and reaches past my bound arms. The alien grabs my shirt and yanks it up to my neck, handling me roughly, but almost as if arms so powerful have no choice.

Alien skin touches my flesh, my gnarled and ropey scars, the Ryph's palm placed flat against my skin. I look down. The Lord's hand covers the three gouges that lead into my surgically repaired knots of flesh. It covers the gouges perfectly.

remember me

"I remember you," I say, the words trapped in my throat. I know that I am dead and that none of this is real, but nightmares aren't escaped so easily. Dreams are where men are free, not nightmares. I can escape no more easily than I can slip my bonds. I am back on Yata, beneath the grand Ryph hive, the last one of my squad alive, sitting in front of the bomb we'd carried across hellish klicks. But I don't set off the bomb. And then a Ryph Lord opens me up. It's the last thing I remember.

"I remember," I whisper. I little more than think the words. This is the same Ryph Lord. He came back to finish what he started.

look

I don't know what I'm supposed to be looking at. The Lord moves his open hand up and presses it against my face. I don't know how I'm supposed to see anything. Rocky gives me some advice:

"Close your eyes, asshole."

I smile. I feel drunk from the GWB. And Rocky still sounds angry at me for drilling a hole through his skull. I only did it to keep him close. Woulda lost him otherwise. Do we have to hurt the ones we love to keep them close?

When I shut my eyes, I see the Ryph Lord standing in front of me, just as he is, but with his hands to his side. And yet I can still feel his hand over my face. My mind relaxes. I am no longer fighting life. This is what we fight. Not death. We fight life. I let go of that, and I can hear Rocky smile.

Your war-mate, who came here on our behalf, she is gone.

Clearer now, I hear the Lord talking. And I see visions beyond him of Scarlett, my old love from the trenches, who came to my beacon and spoke nonsense, who died in my arms, whose lifeless body was carted off by a bounty hunter in all black who never uttered a word.

I think all of this, and by thinking it, I say it. I say Scarlett's name.

War is coming, the Lord says.

"I know," I say. "It's always coming. But you could stop. You don't have to come for us."

Both have to stop. Only we can stop this. Only you can stop this.

I think Scarlett's insanity has leaked into my thoughts. Her nonsense is mixing in with the rest.

A great fleet moves to crush another great fleet. It will pass through here. You will not allow it.

I sense more than just the Ryph's words; I sense his thoughts. His vision. I see ships beyond number. They've been gathering on every moon and every planet, set off in staggered precision, all to meet at once, a million weak lasers concentrated on a single cancer, poised to slice it free.

I see secrets laid bare, secrets the enemy knows. A mass invasion that will fool no one. I see why no ship came to protect us—because it would tip off our enemy. I see why the Ryph want to destroy my beacon. I see why NASA sent a second beacon, because the invasion was too important. I see my being stationed here not to get rid of me but to deploy me. I don't know what to believe.

You and I are the same, the Ryph Lord thinks to me. *You and I and your war-mate and many others. Those who do not wish to fight. Who spare lives. Who hate war. The sad soldiers.*

"Who are you?" I ask. I no longer pretend to be talking. I'm thinking. I feel a deep connection like the one I have with Cricket, and more revelations hit me, more questions. Who is the empath? Maybe it's me.

There are those like me among my people who wish peace. Not enough to take charge. But poised to strike. We made plans with your war-mate. A sudden de-escalation of war. A sudden deceleration of warships.

Deceleration. Bring the war to a sudden stop. Even though I'm seeing the Ryph, I can still feel his palm against my face, the back of my head pressed against the GWB. Knowing I'm already dead fills me with calm. Claire and Cricket are okay. Claire and Cricket are out among the rocks, hiding.

Claire and Cricket are there in the GWB with me.

I can see them, because the Ryph Lord knows about them. They are behind me, bound and gagged, on the other side of the dome, with another Ryph Lord standing guard over them.

I know they are there.

I hear their thoughts, their trembling minds, their terror and fear.

None of us are safe.

I weep into the palm of my enemy.

CHAPTER

32

"Let them go," I silently scream. I think-shout the words. I think-shout them again: "Let them go, you motherfucker!"

Only you can end this.

I open my eyes and twist my face left and right, trying to get free of the Ryph's hand. The claws are pulled away. I try to wiggle around and see if Claire is really there. I feel her like one might feel a presence in a dark room. My hallucinations are creeping into the world of sight and sound. The other Ryph comes into view. The two aliens stare at one another. They are thinking between them. I hear the hiss of a language unknown. I catch only shapes of meanings, the things they visualize. They are arguing. One is afraid. The other has an aura of hope. I feel Cricket there, in my mind. Is she the one we're speaking through? Conduits of conduits. The GWB and my warthen and my pet rock and something Claire opened in my too-tight chest.

"Let them go, and I'll do whatever you want," I say.

The words take shape in the air and across our minds. I feel how to muscle the thoughts into clear form. I realize their voices have been mere whispers in my mind, and that just the same, my words have been mere whispers in theirs. But I am shouting now. I can feel Cricket in my head, a growl of courage slicing through her fear. I give her comfort in return.

"Let them go."

One of the Lords moves out of my vision, but not out of my sight. I can see his mind behind me. I can feel the cosmos through the GWB. I can feel the other beacon and all the rocks and the calm at the core of empty space. The Lord returns, bringing Claire into my view. She is pulled, on her knees, her body sagging, her eyes down at the floor, a bruise on her cheek, jumpsuit ripped, the signs of the struggle she put up, my lovely soldier.

The Lord pulls the gag off Claire's mouth so she can speak.

Rage burns.

There is no keeping it out of their minds.

The aliens look to each other and to me, and I feel as though I should be able to rip my hands free of my bonds and launch into them and kill the indestructible. I am fury and fear and grief. I just want my arms around my love, my body to shield her, and those who wish her harm dead, dead, dead, dead.

peace

This word cannot penetrate.

Peace

I cannot hear it with the sight of Claire in pain.

Peace.

I will not have it.

Please—

And Claire lifts her gaze from the floor, and she sees me, and she smiles. There is a line of blood along the top of her teeth, and she smiles through the pain. "Hey," she mouths. "I love you."

I flood her with love in return, and I see her flinch from the shock of it all. So much at once. Feelings without form. Thoughts without word. What I feel from Cricket when she nuzzles her head against my arm. What I feel from Cricket when she licks my cheek before I can stop her. "No lick," I've said over and over. As futile as it would be for Claire to tell me, "No love." How do you stop loving? You can't. And the war passes through me. The rage dissipates. It's gone. The Lords seem to relax.

"Why haven't they killed us?" Claire asks. Her voice is weak. Her hands are bound together in front of her, and I can see a fingernail that's missing; blood trails down her elbow.

I answer as the thoughts flow between the Lords and through me.

"They want us to murder our own fleet," I say, as startled as Claire to hear the words leave my lips, as we both hear them and process them at the same time. "We've been planning an invasion, and it's passing through here, and they want me to wreck them across those rocks. They want me to turn off the lights in the GWB at twelve past the hour."

Claire shifts from knee to knee, her ankles bound, until she reaches me. The Lords don't stop her. She leans her head against my chest, sags there, trembles a moment before collecting her thoughts.

"Why don't they just do it? What are they waiting for?"

"*I* have to do it," I say. I think I understand what Scarlett wanted and what these Ryph want. Proof of the impossible. Of sheathed claws. To see if we have free will, are not just warring animals. I remember the paperbacks I read that were really written by my enemy. Scarlett said we were the invading aliens. And we are.

"Don't let them use me," Claire whispers. "We're already dead. Don't you dare let them use me to get you to do this. If they're scared of our fleet, then let them get what's fucking coming to them."

I'm watching the Lords while Claire says this. They aren't moving. They're watching us. At least this is real, this conversation with Claire. The thoughts that come next feel just as real.

"They want a trade," I say. "But you aren't part of the bargain."

"Fuck them," Claire hisses.

I stare at the Lords. They're talking to me. I'm talking back. I tell them I understand, but that I don't believe them. That I won't do it. That they'll have to kill us both. That none of this makes sense.

remember

I remember the day I failed to kill the hive. The day I won my medal. The day my belly was opened and I bled on alien soil. The day the Ryph pulled back and no one knows why.

I remember holding Scarlett as she died in my arms. I remember feeling the life leave her body. She came to tell me all of this. She was the messenger. I can feel how much it cost these two Lords to make it here. What they've endured. Rebels on either side, factions who want to put an end to the cycle of violence, to the profits and votes that wars make. I feel a gap in understanding as great as that between my warthen and myself. Alien minds. Minds that know only to mistrust the different, to kill the other. Anything deemed *other*.

"They're serious," I tell Claire. "Our fleet will pass through here today. I can feel it. The war is coming, and they want me to stop it. They want *us* to stop it. It has to be by our hands, don't you see?"

Claire pulls herself upright to sit by me. She places her hands on top of mine. My hands are bound to my legs. I curl a finger around one of her fingers.

"They're using you," she says. "Don't let them."

I listen. I strain to hear everything. It's not me that's an empath, and it's not my warthen who's an empath. It's all of us. But there's a scab over that sense, like the shame of not crying in front of older boys. Something we protect. We dare not share, so we dare not hear. Claire was right: it was something that happened in the trenches. It was something that happened the day I refused to set off that bomb. I'd seen too many children like me die for nothing, and I could feel and hear all those unborn alien minds, not yet scabbed over, still able to listen to the cosmos the way the GWB listens to the cosmos, and they pleaded with me not to do it. They asked for peace. And I gave it to them.

The Ryph have something of this sense. Warthens, too. This great empathy. This rawness. This open wound.

"There are people on both sides who want this war to end," I tell Claire. "There are Ryph like me who are sick of the killing. Some of them are in high places. I think this guy, the larger one, is a prince or something like that. There are others. But so few of us. With no armies. Just unarmed civilians. Shameful pacifists. And even those in power who want to end the war, they don't trust the other side. There's no way to stand down. Nothing anyone will believe."

"What are you talking about?" Claire asks.

"A trade," I say. "An even swap. A gesture to those who don't want to fight anymore, from one side to the other."

"What do they want you to do?"

"I told you, they want me to destroy our fleet. And then they'll destroy their own."

CHAPTER 33

Two hundred and twenty million lives—a settled planet's worth of young men and women—hurtling through space.

I can feel them.

I touch the button that will kill them.

Wires run to the dome behind me that brings me peace.

Hanging from my neck, a small rock trembles in fear.

"Are you sure about this?" Rocky asks.

He knows I'm not.

There's a clock on the wall ticking down the minutes. There's a picture of a lighthouse keeper there as well. He and I stand watch over rocks. We let ships pass without thinking what's in them.

Deep down, I know that I'll do nothing. I've been here before, with the power to annihilate. I keep these thoughts buried deep so the Ryph don't know. One of the Lords stands watch over me. The other has taken Claire to her beacon. There's another switch wired to her GWB, a finger hovering over it missing its nail. There's no way this happens. Claire's last words to me echo in my ears:

"You can't believe them."

Sitting there, contemplating treason upon treason, I nearly laugh out loud at how ridiculous it all seems. It's something I felt on the front before, when the kinetic rounds were coming down from orbital artillery and throwing up geysers of hot earth and shrapnel, and somehow you're wading through it all and handing death to those on the other side, and you just have to laugh. The orange blossoms of HE rounds, and the curving tracers like glowing and screaming bees, and the howling jets diving through atmo and dropping hell. The fact that you are alive is hilarious. The fact that the universe can come to this, that anyone finds it normal, is comically absurd.

I remember Scarlett, naïve Scarlett, the equally absurd. I remember the bounty on her life. I remember the risks she took to get to me and the impossible task she expected of me. I remember, vividly, that she knew things she shouldn't have. She knew what had happened on Yata. She forced me to admit it, but she already knew.

Looking up at the Ryph, whose hand matches my scars, I think about the fact that he was there. He's the only other soul who knows what happened that day. This explains how Scarlett knew. It's because he knew Scarlett. They were working together. I see this in his thoughts, and he sees what I'm thinking. I see that this is a test.

"They don't know if we're capable of kindness," I tell Rocky. "We can't speak their language, can't think to each other like they do."

"You mean they don't talk crazy like you do," Rocky says. "You know I'm not real. None of this is real."

"I think it is," I say.

I touch the button that will kill my beacon to reassure myself of what's real. This button is real. One press, and the greatest army of humans ever assembled disappears.

"This is what's wrong with me," I say. And Rocky listens. "It's why I feel the gwib. It's why I don't want to go on. It's too much."

"Listen to Claire," Rocky says. "Listen to her."

I shake my head. "No. This is right. She should listen to *me*. They want to see if we're worth saving or if we're too dangerous to have around. I want to see the same from them."

"And then what?" Rocky asks.

I rest my head against the dome. I can feel the cosmos breathe, can feel the black hole at the galaxy's core pulse. There is a rift between the two, between pulse and breath. A warring divide. I sense Claire over there, near the other GWB. Two antennas. I reach out to her, feel her anger and fear, the fact that I've betrayed her. I feel her bound arms, Cricket trembling by her side, the Ryph Lord who will push the button when I tell him to, if Claire won't. They just need to see what we're capable of. Will one be enough? Just me? I think of Claire's spreadsheet with all the checkmarks and no Xs. That's data. What will the Ryph conclude if only one of us goes through with it? And what if the Ryph sitting elsewhere don't go through with their end? Will I be killing my people or their people? Is there a difference?

Is this what they want me to see, to feel? That there is no difference? That life is life. Is this the test?

Two hundred and twenty million lives. Even more on their side. Over half a billion souls. Tearing along through the cosmos at each other. They are already dead, all those young men and women. I tell myself this, and I tell it to Claire. Half a billion now or billions and billions more later. No end in sight. Don't generals and admirals make this call? Don't they kill our boys and girls every day? When I was sane, I bawled over the death of eight human souls, the crew of a cargo bound for Vega. What am I thinking now? I go back and forth, like a man crazed then sane, like a finger punching in three digits of a lock code with confidence, then hovering over the fourth, a man who can only kill himself so far, who can't quite go all the way. I hear Scarlett yelling at me from the beyond to do this, to end this war, to be brave.

Just a few minutes to decide. All those boys and girls. The smell of gun oil. Anticipation. Dreaded Sundays. Fathers clutching their dead pups and old hearts and strong wives and crying for the first time in how long? How fucking long?

"I'm gonna do it, Rocky. For Scarlett."

"No—"

"For Hank."

"Please—"

"If there's a chance, just a chance—"

"And then what?"

It's Claire speaking. It's her thoughts. She's crying too. She taught me how.

"Do you love me?" I ask.

There is quiet.

Tears.

Fear.

". . . yes."

"There are good people, Claire. There are enough good people on either side. You and me—"

She sees into my thoughts. I hear her laugh behind those tears. I feel the word:

politics—?

"Maybe," I say. "Maybe. Something more than this. Something less cowardly."

The ships are near. A wall of ships. Designed to break through and hit sector eight all at once, to overwhelm with the element of surprise, but everyone sees this coming. Just as everyone must see the coordinated response from the other side. Some of the people working with the rebels helped plan this, helped on both sides, helped line them up like sitting ducks.

I look to the Ryph Lord who nearly took my life. "I'm trusting you," I tell him. "I'm trusting you."

He makes a sign with his claws. I don't know what it means, but I can read his thoughts. I am an empath, a dangerous thing. I didn't ask to have my soul torn open, or my belly, or my goddamn life. I didn't ask for any of this. But it was handed to me. And the only thing that ends a war like this is trust, release, love for those we hate, arms around those who would kill us, forgiveness, forgiveness, forgiveness.

"Do you love me, Claire?"

"I do."

She is shaking with tears, listening to me, knowing the time is here, that it'll be with her or without her. It'll be her clawless hand or the Ryph's. But she knows now, either way, what my hand will do.

Rocky is gone. Clarity takes his place. All my brothers and sisters, and why is this act so unthinkable when my orders on Yata were the exact same? Who gets to make that choice? Right now, I do.

The moment.

Here.

War, coming.

They'll kill me for this.

When I deserve a medal.

I pull my head away from the GWB, want to feel what I feel, want my mind clear, want to allow those memories of war to creep in, creep back, torment me for a sliver of time longer, before I pull a trigger of horrible pacifism, a button of treason, those ships traveling too fast to stop, and the world is aglow, Claire crying for what we've done, the two of us, a million stars coming to life and full of death, and across the module the portholes facing out toward Yata glow as in the distance a similar wall of flame erupts, more stars appearing briefly and burning out, this violent, terrible, treasonous, glorious eruption of peace.

Note from the Author

I know it is fiction to imagine, but what would happen if we stood on the rubble of attacks against us, whether literal or figurative, physical or emotional, personal or political, and we chose to forgive rather than escalate? What does that world look like? Maybe we'll never know. But I like to pretend.

· Epilogue ·

The Ryph turbines and the navy jet engines scream in harmony. Steel cables hang taut from two craft built for dogfighting but now converted for commercial use. Swinging from the end of the cables, and hovering over the shore of the Chesapeake, is an old lighthouse. The stonework is intact, but the crown and foundation will take rebuilding.

I've spent countless hours staring at a picture of this lighthouse, a giant wave crashing up its spine, an old man standing there back when those rusted stumps were the stanchions for steel railings. I can almost see the ghost of the old man there, smiling at me.

When I got back to Earth from the Yata Peace Council, the first thing I did was track the old lighthouse down. I found her like a battered old soldier standing out in the waves, the foundation ready to go at any moment. Soon, she would have been lost for good. And so I decided to save her. I did the opposite of what those old wreckers used to do who demolished for profit. It took calling in some favors, but there's very little a planetary governor-elect and old war hero can't do.

The crew marrying the old lighthouse to its new foundation are a motley bunch. The foreman in charge of the project is Tryndian. There are two Hokos on his crew, three humans, and one of the pilots up there is a Ryph. A Ryph on Earth. Races that grew up warring among themselves and with each other now concentrate on the job at hand. And the job at claw, I suppose.

Reading my mind, Claire slips her hand into mine. Her other hand rests on her belly, which is full as the moon. Ten paces away, Cricket slinks into the tall grass, only her tail visible, stalking something only she can see.

Sometimes I feel overwhelmed with contentment. Sometimes I question what I did. Laughter and sobs still orbit too close to one another for comfort. But it won't be my challenge to forgive my actions. That's a test for the next generation. It shouldn't be easy; that's the whole point. I remember what I felt after the attack on Delphi. I remember the anger that caused me to enlist. The last thing in my mind was forgiveness. With the end of the war, someone tallied the total cost of all those little decisions, and it came to just over eighteen billion dead.

Half a billion of those are on me.

Claire pulls me close, places her hand on the back of my hand, holding my palm where the baby is kicking, is trying to distract my thoughts and redirect them to life. To renewal. The old lighthouse settles onto its foundation, the work crew tight and organized. I can feel the lacework of scars beneath Claire's dress. She's been trying to convince me that the boy should have my name. I haven't liked the idea. I don't want him to turn out like me.

But maybe he won't. Maybe he'll do my name proud. And so I squeeze Claire's hand and I agree. I test it out, whispering my own name in Claire's ear, but the syllables are lost in a sudden breeze, and the soft sound is carried far out to sea, where it will swirl and mingle and be lost and present for all the rest of time.

www.hughhowey.com
@hughhowey